The Compound

The Compound
The Compound Trilogy – Book 1

Claire Thompson

Edited by Jae Ashley & Donna Fisk

Copyright © 2019 Claire Thompson

All rights reserved

ISBN: 9781482302493

Chapter 1

"Offer yourself. Stop holding back. Give it to me!" The flogger struck her body with so much force Alexis was knocked out of position. She stumbled forward into the two men standing just in front of her who were watching the scene with gaping mouths and visible erections.

They both reached for her with hot hands, catching and steadying her. Alexis twisted back to face Arthur as she pulled away from the strangers. She was panting, her skin on fire, her nipples hard as cherry pits. She wrapped her arms around her torso and licked her lips, wishing the men clustered around them would disappear.

"Focus," Arthur snapped, his dark eyes blazing. "Nothing matters but you and me and this." He held up the heavy-tressed leather flogger. "Get back in position. Now."

With a nod, Alexis turned again, facing the men whose eyes moved hungrily over her body, which was covered only by a pair of black silk bikini panties. She grasped her left wrist with her right hand, extending her arms high over her head. She planted her bare feet firmly on the floor, shoulder-width apart.

Arthur came up close behind her and she had to resist a sudden impulse to lean back into him. He reached for her long ponytail, which he lifted and placed over her shoulder and out of the way. Alexis almost smiled — Arthur was always so thoughtful.

The flogger struck her ass, a heavy, thudding thwack that made her tense her muscles in order to stay upright. Stinging ribbons of leather struck her back and shoulders. The burn on her skin was matched by the heat in her cunt, which was stoked by each stinging cut of the lash.

She was close. She could feel it. She was almost there, almost to that point where she could let go and soar, becoming one with the leather, one with the pain, one with the pleasure of pure, sweet submission...

"Jesus, she's so fucking hot. What I wouldn't give to bury my cock in that."

The words distracted her, uttered by one of the gawkers that always surrounded her at every scene.

She felt herself being pulled back to earth by the snickers and muttered agreement of the spectators. She could smell their body odor—sweat, stale cigarette smoke and cheap cologne. She opened her eyes, glaring at them, twitching and jerking as the flogger thudded against her.

Another hard blow made her stumble forward, her concentration shattered, her balance off. She jerked away from the greedy hands of the men waiting to catch her and whirled toward Arthur, her anger at herself misdirected toward him. "I can't do this. I can't!"

"You won't," he retorted, frowning, but he put down the flogger and reached for her robe, which he draped around her shoulders.

"Show's over," he said to the men still crowded around them. The group parted as he led Alexis past them toward the juice bar. She perched gingerly on the stool, her ass still stinging from the flogging.

She sipped fresh grapefruit juice over crushed ice, watching Arthur out of the corner of her eye. He had ordered coffee, into which he was stirring several spoons of sugar. He was frowning into the cup.

"What?" she demanded, feeling defensive.

"You know what. That scene back there. When are you going to move past whatever it is that's holding you back?"

"Maybe I can't." Alexis snapped angrily. "Maybe I'm just a player, a masochistic exhibitionist with something to prove."

Arthur looked at her, his kind, hound dog eyes searching hers. "Do you really believe that?"

Alexis shrugged miserably, looking away. "I don't know. I'm starting to think so. I get to a certain point and I just, I don't know, I shut down."

Arthur nodded. "It's not so easy here in this public venue. Maybe we should..."

Alexis shook her head firmly. It wasn't the first time one or the other of them had entertained the idea of meeting at a motel to try their scenes in private. Alexis knew in her bones that would be a bad move for both of them, and she reminded Arthur of this now. "No. You know you would hate yourself if you did something behind Naomi's back. And that would make you hate me, too. I couldn't bear that, Arthur, losing what we have now."

Arthur nodded, unconsciously playing with his wedding ring. His wife of twenty- six years was not at all into the BDSM scene, but understood Arthur's need to explore his dominant side. After years of failed experimentation, and Arthur sneaking around to get his needs met, they'd come to a compromise that he could scene all he wanted at the BDSM clubs, as long as he kept it there, and kept his cock in his pants.

Though twenty-five years Alexis's senior, Arthur was still a handsome man, in a grizzled, rough sort of way, and she found it romantic that he was so obviously still in love with his wife, despite their sexual differences. Alexis never wanted to be the one to come between them, no matter how attracted she might be to her favorite scene partner.

The scene, as much as she hated to admit it, was getting old. But what was left?

Maybe it was because she was about to turn thirty, and she'd recently been taking stock of her life. On the surface she looked like a Manhattan success story—already a junior partner at a top CPA firm, making good money in a job she found both challenging and satisfying. She had a great apartment in a good neighborhood near Central Park, where she jogged each morning before work to keep herself fit and toned.

She'd had several serious relationships in her twenties, the first two vanilla, the last one this past year with a dominant man she thought she might be in love with, but it had fizzled out. She'd met him at this very BDSM club, and had been excited by the promise of a 24/7 D/s relationship, but their ideas of what that entailed hadn't matched.

Alexis longed to connect with what she believed was her inner submissive core, while James, it turned out, was more into the trappings of the scene—like having her wear a collar and meet him naked in the foyer when he got home from work. He wanted her to call him Master, and wake him up with a blow job each morning. He was good with a whip, but somehow always seemed to stop just before she reached that place that she felt, in her bones, would somehow set her free.

She had come to realize it was more of a sexy game for him than anything. She rarely felt that tremor of fear and desire that infused her sexual fantasies with a blaze of erotic heat. She never truly submitted to him, not with her heart and soul, as she dreamed of doing with the right man, if such a man existed. In the end, she realized she had wanted more than he could give. Yet when he'd gone she was lonelier than ever, left to wonder if what she craved was unattainable.

"Earth to Alexis." Arthur was regarding her with a quizzical smile.

"Oh, sorry. I was drifting."

Arthur studied her a moment and then said, "You're sad." It wasn't a question, but a statement, and Alexis nodded, surprised to find a tear rolling down her cheek. She wiped it away, annoyed with herself. She was at the club to have fun, to forget, not to wallow in her misery.

As if sensing her embarrassment, Arthur turned back to his coffee. He lifted the cup and took a long sip. "You know," he said, "I've been thinking for a while now that you need more than you can get at a club like this. You need someone who can break past those barriers you place in your own way."

"Tell me about it," she agreed morosely. "You saw how great things worked out with James."

Arthur smiled kindly. "James isn't the only dominant fish in the sea, my dear. In fact, between you and me, I'm not sure he's dominant at all. He's more of a slap and tickle kind of guy. I never thought he was right for you."

"Ha." Alexis grinned in spite of herself. "Well, thanks for the heads up on that one."

"Like you would have listened to me," he rejoined. "You were sure you'd found 'the one', remember?" He used his fingers to put quotations around the words.

"Yeah," she admitted with a sigh. "I don't know if such a person exists, to tell you the truth. At least not for me. I'm scared to admit it, but I think I'm the problem, and that really sucks, you know?"

"I might have a solution for your problem," Arthur said slowly, turning on his stool to face her. "There's a place I heard about recently, located upstate. It's a BDSM training facility. It's pretty intense, from what I understand. The primary focus is on slave training. Maybe the trainers there could help you get past whatever it is that's holding you back."

Alexis felt a chill move down her spine, part fear, part thrill. Just the words slave training sent a tremor of excitement and longing through her entire being. "Tell me more," she urged, leaning toward him. "Is there a website?"

Arthur shook his head. "No website. It's a very private place. Word of mouth only. Off the grid, I guess you'd say. You need a referral. I know someone who knows someone. If you were interested, I could probably get an email address for you to at least start the process."

"It sounds intriguing. But upstate? How far? I don't have a car, you know. Not to mention I work sixty hours a week."

"Well, if you were serious about it, you'd have to take off from work. It's not some part time commitment, Alexis. You live there during the training. We're talking full immersion, 24/7. I believe the initial commitment is a month."

"A month? How could I ever take a month off work?" Even as she said this, she knew she could get a month if she wanted. In fact, just the week before, Jenny Olsen, her friend in human resources, had called Alexis into her office, handing her a printout of her accrued vacation time. "I wanted to give you the heads up. You have six unused weeks of vacation time. There's a new policy coming down the pike — starting next year, whatever you don't use, you lose. My advice is to take your time now. You know the senior guys will get priority once word's out about the change."

Arthur raised his eyebrows. "When was the last time you took a vacation? I mean a real vacation, not a long weekend? Tax season is over." He shrugged. "Maybe you should find out more about it before you make a decision. Maybe it's more than you could handle anyway."

"Get me the email address," she snapped. Arthur grinned and she grinned back, aware he'd set her up. The minute he'd suggested it was more than she could handle, she'd bristled, taking the challenge.

Later that night alone in bed, Alexis reached for her trusty vibrator. She squeezed a dollop of lubricant onto the head and nestled the phallus between her labia. Flicking it to a low setting, she closed her eyes, surrendering herself to her favorite fantasies of being bound and controlled by a strong, sexy guy who took her past her limits with his touch, his words, his whip, his kiss...

She is tied with strips of red silk, knotted around her wrists and ankles, pulling her into a human X. Her body is bathed in sweat, her dark hair flying as she twists and moans with each cutting kiss of the single tail he is flicking over her body. She is panting, nearly crying, biting her lip to keep from begging. "Stop, don't stop, never stop..." Dropping the whip at last, he moves to stand in front of her, taking her face in his hands and kissing her lips, slipping his tongue into her mouth, while his hard, insistent fingers push into her wetness.

She is on his bed, a large bed with soft sheets. He looms over her, his body hard and strong as he eases his huge cock inside her. "What are you?"

"The place where your cock goes, Sir."

"I own you."

"Yesssss..."

She flicked the vibrator to high and slid it inside herself. The vibrations whirred against her engorged clit, the phallus throbbing inside her. As his hard cock pummeled her to orgasm, Alexis tried to see the man's face in her fantasy, but there was only shadow, and then even that slipped away.

With a sigh, she turned off the toy and eased it from her pussy, dropping it onto the small towel by her bed so she'd remember to wash it in the morning. She closed her eyes and sighed, waiting for sleep to claim her.

But instead of slipping into dreams, her conversation with Arthur kept coming back to her. The idea sounded sexy and a little dangerous.

Without realizing what she was doing, Alexis found her fingers had slipped back between her legs, sliding into the wetness still left from the lubricant and her own lust. She rubbed herself, imagining her breasts pressed against rough stone as a whip struck her again and again. Her wrists were cuffed into manacles set into the stone, her legs stretched wide and secured at the ankle.

The man drops his whip at last and presses his hard body against her flayed, stinging back. She feels his hands spreading her ass, and then the press of his impossibly hard cock against her nether entrance. He eases himself inside her, moving slowly, but still she feels as if she's being split in two by his girth. His fingers dig into her hips as he begins to thrust in and out of her ass. "Someday," he murmurs, his lips touching her ear, "I will fuck your cunt. When you prove yourself worthy, when you submit without reservation, when you give of yourself completely."

Alexis moaned aloud, arching her hips, her

fingers a flurry as she brought herself to a second orgasm, more powerful than the first. She lay still, a light sweat cooling on her skin, until the rapid tapping of her heart slowly subsided.

She heard a pinging sound on her iPhone and reached for it from the nightstand beside her bed. She had an email from Arthur. The subject read: The Compound. The body of the email consisted of an email address: Mistress.Miriam@gmail.com, along with a note from Arthur that she'd been cleared as a possible applicant. Just tell them the truth, he'd written, about what you're looking for, and that you'd like more information about the program offered through The Compound. Don't wuss out, Alexis. This is your chance. Take it. Good luck! Arthur.

Before she could lose her resolve, Alexis copied the email address and pasted it into a new email.

Dear Mistress Miriam,

My name is Alexis Stewart...

~*~

It had been two weeks since she first began her email correspondence with Mistress Miriam. The initial exchange had been conversational in tone, with Alexis being as honest as she could in expressing her needs, experience and goals. She'd been surprised but pleased to learn there was no cost to attend the program.

Alexis had completed a lengthy questionnaire about her experience in the scene, likes, dislikes, goals, hard limits, etc. She'd undergone a complete physical and blood work to prove she was in good health and disease-free. She was impressed when Mistress Miriam told her all staff members at The Compound were held to the same high standards. Alexis had been thrilled when Mistress Miriam told her she appeared to be a good candidate for The Compound. She put in for and was approved for a full month's vacation time at work.

Arthur drove her the two hours from the city. As he pulled up in front of the large main building of what appeared to have once been a horse farm, Alexis experienced the same clutch of excitement and fear as when she'd been shipped off to sleep away camp as a child. Arthur gave her a quick farewell kiss on the cheek. "Good luck, kiddo."

There was still the face-to-face interview to undergo before she was formally accepted into the program. "If by some chance we decide you aren't right for the program," Mistress Miriam had assured her in her last email, "we have a driver who can give you a lift back to the city. No need to make your ride wait."

Alexis grabbed her bag and went up to the large front door. Before she could even lift the heavy brass knocker, the door was opened by a tall young man dressed in only a black thong, a thick leather collar secured at his throat by a padlock. He didn't speak, but only nodded toward her as he reached down to take her suitcase. He led her into a brightly lit office space with large bay windows that looked out over a huge swimming pool and beautiful flower gardens.

An imposing woman in her late thirties stood as they entered, moving from behind her desk to take Alexis's hand in hers. "Welcome, Alexis. I'm Mistress Miriam." Her voice fit her perfectly, low and smooth, with just the hint of a British accent. She was a striking woman, with lustrous dark hair falling in waves to her shoulders and eyes a vivid blue. She wore a tailored red silk jacket that revealed a hint of bare nipple beneath, over red leather pants that looked soft as butter. She radiated confidence and power. She exuded raw sexuality, and for a nearly irresistible second, Alexis had the impulse to lean forward and kiss those full, sensuous lips.

"You may wait outside, Josh," Mistress Miriam said, turning her attention for a moment to the male slave. He nodded and stepped out, closing the door silently behind him.

Mistress Miriam leaned against the edge of the desk and regarded Alexis with a cool gaze. Without any preamble, she said simply, "Take off your clothes, everything except panties."

Though she'd been expecting this, or something like it, Alexis's mouth went suddenly dry. Under Mistress Miriam's cool gaze, she stood and reached for the

buttons of her blouse, praying her hands wouldn't shake. Her eyes flicked toward a black leather flogger and a long, thin rattan cane that rested on the desk beside Mistress Miriam. Alexis let the blouse fall from her shoulders as she kicked off her sandals. She unbuckled her belt, opened her pants and slid them down her legs. Finally, taking a breath, she reached back and undid the clasps to her bra.

"Fold your things and place them on the desk," Mistress Miriam instructed. "Then stand at attention, hands behind your head." Alexis reached for her things, placing them on the desk as instructed. Lifting her arms, she locked her fingers behind her head and waited, hoping she didn't look as nervous as she felt.

"Stand up straight," Mistress Miriam snapped. "Breasts out."

Alexis put her shoulders back, thrusting her size C breasts forward, willing away the heat that wanted to climb into her face. She wasn't shy about her body, but something about Mistress Miriam's piercing gaze made her want to cover herself. She forced herself to resist the impulse.

Mistress Miriam stood, moving to stand directly in front of Alexis. "You stated on the questionnaire that you believe you are submissive, but you've had trouble reaching the inner core of that submission. In your essay you questioned if you might only be sexually masochistic, and not really capable of true submission. Do I have that correct, Alexis?"

"Yes, Mistress."

"Are you obedient?"

In the right circumstances, Alexis thought. With the right man. Glancing at the gorgeous Mistress

Miriam, she suddenly wondered — with the right woman? Aloud she replied, "Yes, Mistress."

Mistress Miriam stepped back. She cupped Alexis's left breast, lifting it and letting it fall. She pinched both Alexis's nipples with her sharp, blood red nails. Alexis pressed her lips together to keep from crying out, her eyes on Mistress Miriam's face, her hands locked obediently behind her head. When Mistress Miriam finally let go, Alexis's nipples were erect and throbbing.

Mistress Miriam put a hand over Alexis's crotch, and Alexis almost stepped back, embarrassed to be touched so intimately by another woman, especially when she knew her panties were damp from the exchange between them so far. She stopped herself in time, determined to prove she was obedient, though she couldn't stop her gasp when Mistress Miriam slipped a finger into her panties.

"If we accept you, this will have to go." Mistress Miriam tugged lightly at Alexis's pubic hair. "We have a specialist in full body waxing. All our trainees must be smooth and completely accessible at all times. Is that a problem?"

"No, Mistress," Alexis replied.

Mistress Miriam returned to the desk, though she didn't sit down. "Which do you prefer, the flogger or the cane?"

"The flogger," Alexis said immediately. It was no contest — she hated to be caned. It held none of the sweet, thuddy sensuousness of a flogging. It just plain fucking hurt.

"Ah. Then we'll use the cane." One side of Mistress Miriam's mouth lifted in a cruel smile.

If she had said the cane, would Mistress Miriam have picked the flogger? Probably. Though then again, probably not. Somehow Alexis sensed she would have known she was lying. How had Mistress Miriam managed to hone in on the one thing Alexis had a hard time with? Was it some kind of sadist's sixth sense? She could take a single tail, she could even handle a bull whip. But the cane — with its stingy bite, and that scary whooshing sound just before it struck the skin — sent a chill down her back just thinking about it.

You got this far, she admonished herself. Don't screw it up now.

"Face the chair, bend over and grab the arms. Legs wide, ass out. Oh, and take off

those panties."

Alexis pulled her panties down and stepped out of them, adding them to the folded pile of her clothing. Taking a breath, she turned toward the chair. She bent forward and gripped the smooth wooden arms, steadying herself as she spread her legs. Her heart was beating a mile a minute, but she was determined. She could do this. She would do this.

She could hear Mistress Miriam moving behind her. When she felt the light tap of the cane against her ass, she stiffened, but managed to remain still. By turning her head, she could just see Mistress Miriam out of the corner of her eye, standing back and to the side.

"Eyes straight ahead," Mistress Miriam snapped, punctuating her words with the first real strike of the cane. Alexis gasped in pain, gripping the chair arms hard as she struggled to maintain her composure. Several more whacks followed in quick succession, each one landing just below the last. As the cane moved lower, covering the fleshier part of Alexis's ass, she found herself better able to tolerate the stinging blows.

Until the one that struck just where her ass met her thighs. It was harder than the others, preceded by that sudden, terrifying whoosh and then a searing, biting flash of pain that pushed a cry from Alexis's lips.

She lifted her head, her eyes momentarily blinded by tears. Stop fighting it. Flow with the pain. Become one with it. She could almost hear Arthur admonishing her, and she tried to do just that, though she'd never really understood the concept, not on a gut level. Another blow caught her on the hip and she gritted her teeth, not sure she could take much more of this.

She looked out the window, thinking maybe she could distract herself enough with the view to at least get through this caning without making a fool of herself by screaming, or worse, turning around and grabbing the fucking thing from Mistress Miriam's hands and breaking it clean in two.

And then she saw him.

The pool had been empty when she'd first entered the office, but now someone was swimming in it— muscular back and powerful shoulders moving through the water and then a head lifting, shaking the water from auburn hair that glittered like dark, wet gold in the sunlight.

The man swam to the opposite side of the pool and leaned back, lifting his arms to rest against the edge, revealing his smooth, bronzed chest. His jaw was square, his nose prominent. He seemed to be staring directly at her.

The cane struck her ass again and again, but somehow, with her eyes on the handsomest man she'd ever seen in her life, Alexis found herself able to tolerate the blows. She began to breathe more deeply, her tightly-clenched muscles easing. She kept her gaze on him, drawing strength and courage from his handsome visage as she drank in the masculine curves of his body. Would he be her trainer?

Please, please, please, let him be my trainer.

Suddenly Alexis felt Mistress Miriam's cool fingers tracing the welts she had raised along Alexis's ass and thighs. When the hand slid between her legs, Alexis gasped, but maintained her position. She looked again at the Greek god still leaning back against the side of the pool, and imagined it was his hand touching her pussy, probing her entrance, sliding over her clit.

When Mistress Miriam began to rub and tease

her, Alexis kept her focus on the man in the pool. The caning, though it had hurt like hell, had aroused Alexis, as all erotic pain did. That arousal, along with the vision of the man in the pool, and the realization that a gorgeous, dominant woman was touching her, all combined to make Alexis tremble and moan, teetering suddenly on the edge of an orgasm.

She felt Mistress Miriam moving closer, her small breasts touching Alexis's bare back. Her perfume was intoxicating, her touch a velvet heat at Alexis's cunt.

"Come for me, Alexis."

She did, keeping her eyes on the handsome man until they fluttered shut in the last throes of a powerful orgasm. She sank to her knees in front of the chair, her body shaking, her heart beating fast, her breath ragged in her throat.

When she finally regained enough control to pull herself upright, she turned to face Mistress Miriam, who was seated once more behind the desk, the cane back in its place beside the flogger.

"You'll do," she said, a small smile playing over her lips. "Sit down and we'll go over the contract."

With a glance at her clothing, Alexis settled gingerly on the edge of the chair, her ass still smarting from the cane. Mistress Miriam pushed a piece of paper over the desk toward her. "This is the contract. Take your time. Read it carefully. It basically gives us full discretion to train you as we see fit. The minimum stay is one month, and by signing the contract, you give up all rights and control. You will become a Compound slave, and as such subject to the dictates and control of every Master and Mistress here. You will be assigned to a specific trainer, who will have primary responsibility for your training.

"Once training is deemed complete, if you're interested, there is a significant market of Dominants interested in procuring trained sex slaves and submissives for their own use. You would be amply compensated, if that's a route you choose, and the fees for placement are handled by the Master who procured you. Otherwise you are free to return to your life. Some slaves choose to remain at The Compound after training, if there's a place for them."

Mistress Miriam smiled. "But I'm getting ahead of myself. First things first. Read the contract. Take your time. Just be aware, once you sign, there's no going back. You are committed to the month, with no recourse to leave the program. I'll give you a few minutes alone. Can I bring you something? Coffee, a cold drink?"

Alexis swallowed, her mind reeling with what she was about to do. "Water would be good," she managed, realizing she was in fact quite thirsty. She picked up the single page, trying to focus on the words. She couldn't resist turning back toward the window, but the man who had been swimming was gone.

She read the terms of the contract, which were as Mistress Miriam had stated. If Alexis signed, she basically agreed to give up all rights to her person for the duration of the one-month training period. Once she signed the contract, she would be expected to comply with every dictate of The Compound staff. She would agree to submit to physical punishment and training, including but not limited to whipping, flogging, caning, bondage, sexual torture and stimulation, orgasm training and control, and sexual interactions of all kinds with her trainer and whoever the trainer deemed appropriate in the course of her training. She thought back to the first night Arthur had brought up the idea, and realized her fantasies, as wild as she had thought them at the time, weren't at all far from the truth.

She lifted the pen Mistress Miriam had left for her, hesitating over the signature line. She didn't have to sign. No one was holding a gun to her head. It wasn't too late — she could still walk away. This was her choice, and hers alone.

Her ass still stinging from the bite of the cane, her cunt still throbbing from the intense orgasm she'd experienced under Mistress Miriam's direction, Alexis asked herself if she was ready for this. Did she have the courage to go through with it? Did she want to?

She thought about the years she'd been alone. Even when she was dating guys or involved in a relationship, she always felt, at her core, alone. Her email discussions with Mistress Miriam had clarified what she'd really always known — she was a submissive who hadn't yet found the right person or situation in which to explore and embrace that submission. Now she was being offered an amazing opportunity, and if she walked away, she knew she would regret it for the rest of her life.

The office door opened and Alexis turned, expecting to see Mistress Miriam with her glass of water. Instead it was the man she'd seen in the pool, dressed now in a black button-down shirt rolled to his muscular, tanned forearms, and black jeans. Up close he was even handsomer, his eyes the same coppery color as his hair, his skin kissed by the sun.

"You must be Alexis," he said, handing her the water. His eyes moved over her naked body and the blush she'd managed to keep at bay under Mistress Miriam's scrutiny now bloomed over her chest and cheeks. "Mistress Miriam has been detained for a few moments. I'm Master Paul."

Alexis took the water, electrified as their fingers touched. Please, please, please let him be my trainer.

She realized she was still holding the pen, the contract as yet unsigned. Setting down the water, she leaned over the paper and scrawled her signature on the indicated line.

There! It was done.

She leaned back in her chair, turning toward Master Paul with a nervous smile. He smiled back, his teeth even and white, his eyes crinkling at the corners suggesting a man who laughed often. "I'll take that." He held out his hand, and Alexis passed over the signed contract.

"Welcome to The Compound." He glanced at his

watch. "Master John, your trainer, should be here shortly to meet you."

Chapter 2

Mistress Miriam appeared a moment later, a man behind her. Like Master Paul, the guy was also dressed in black, a thick cotton T-shirt that hugged a muscular torso and showed off powerfully muscled arms. He stood a little over six feet, with dark blond hair that fell in a thatch over his forehead. He had round blue eyes and a long, elegant nose over thin lips. Tall and well built, he was handsome in a Ken Barbie doll sort of way. He stared unblinkingly at Alexis, reminding her of an owl focused intently on its prey. He moved his eyes in a slow, brazen sweep over Alexis's naked form, making her feel somehow more naked than she'd been a moment before.

"Alexis, this is Master John. He will be your trainer during your stay here," Mistress Miriam said. Alexis cast a longing look in Master Paul's direction, biting her tongue to keep from begging Mistress Miriam to assign her to him instead of the formidable Master John.

She knew better than that, however, aware it would not be a good start. She wasn't here to pick up some hot guy, but to learn about herself and her submissive potential. All the trainers at The Compound were purported to be top-notch. Her first step in this process was to trust that they knew better than she what was needed to help her reach her goal.

With the barest of nods in her direction, Master Paul disappeared from the room, leaving Alexis with Mistress Miriam and her new trainer. Mistress Miriam returned to her desk. "From this moment forward," she said to Alexis, "you belong to Master John. He will oversee every aspect of your physical care and well-being. He has complete authority over your training. His word is law. Do you understand, Alexis?"

"Yes, Mistress," Alexis replied, the full extent of what she'd signed on for really sinking in now. She glanced at Master John, who was still looking her over with that owl-like gaze, his thin lips compressed in what seemed to her a disapproving line.

"Let's go," he said abruptly. "Once you're properly groomed, I'll assess your strengths and weaknesses, and develop a training regimen tailored to your needs."

Master John held out his hand. But when Alexis moved forward to take it, he reached instead for the back of her neck, grabbing her in a viselike hold and pushing her ahead of him out the door.

Startled, Alexis tried to twist back to Mistress Miriam, but Master John's grip was firm, and he quickly propelled her from the room, through the front hall of the main building and out the door, her suitcase and the pile of her clothing still in Mistress Miriam's office.

The summer day was muggy, and the stones of the path on which they walked were hot beneath her bare feet. Master John, his hand still on the back of Alexis's neck, stopped her as they approached the sidewalk and in a moment she saw why. A woman in a black tank top and a flowing black skirt was leading a naked man on a leash. As they approached, Alexis saw that he had no trace of hair on his body. Her eyes flickered over his denuded cock and balls as the couple passed her. As they walked away, Alexis caught a glimpse of the man's back and ass. The skin was covered in welts, both fresh and fading, and Alexis felt her own recently caned skin tingle in sympathy.

Master John led her in the opposite direction to a long, single story building located behind the main house. "This used to be the stables," he said tersely, confirming Alexis's earlier impression that the place had once been a horse farm. "Now it's the slave quarters. This is where all trainees stay."

His hand still on her neck, Master John opened the door on the side of the building and pushed her inside. The place had the feel of a dormitory, with doors on either side of a long hallway. A few of the doors were ajar, and Alexis could see a single bed and a small bureau in each tiny, windowless room. Master John led her past these to the end of the hall, which opened onto a large communal bathroom complete with showers and toilets, though, Alexis noted, there were no doors or curtains to offer privacy. There was also what looked like a doctor's exam table, a narrow high trolley on wheels beside it loaded with various pots and jars.

Toward the back of the space Alexis saw a young African-American woman wearing a thong similar to the one Josh had been wearing, her breasts bare. She was on her knees on a black rubber mat beside a huge sunken bathtub, her back straight, her hands resting lightly on her thighs. Like Josh, she wore a thick leather collar with a padlock at the throat.

"This is Marta," Master John said, nodding toward the kneeling young woman as he finally let go of Alexis's neck, "one of our fulltime slave staff. She will bathe and groom you and then take you to your room. You will wait there on your knees in an at- ease position for my inspection. You will not move from that position until I arrive. Are we quite clear on this?"

Alexis swallowed hard and nodded. Master John's visage darkened, a frown appearing beneath the unblinking eyes. "Lesson one. You will always answer a direct question, and you will address me with the proper respect."

"Yes, Sir. Yes, Master John," Alexis replied quickly, embarrassed.

He turned toward Marta. "Full grooming. You have one hour." He glanced pointedly at a large clock set over the sinks.

"Yes, Master John," the woman replied softly.

With a brusque nod, the man turned on his

booted heel and left the room.

Marta rose from the mat in a single, fluid movement, like a ballet dancer, Alexis thought. Her breasts were small and round, her dark nipples large in comparison, and pierced with gold hoops. "Come," she said. "We haven't much time."

Alexis approached her, not sure what was expected. "First, I'll wash your hair," Marta said. "Then to the waxing station. Have you ever been waxed?"

Alexis shook her head. Her trepidation must have showed on her face because Marta laughed kindly. "Relax. It's not too terribly painful. I'm quite good at it. I did it for a living before I came to The Compound. But we have to hurry. An hour doesn't give us much time."

Alexis climbed into the steaming water. Marta squirted lavender-scented soap onto a washcloth and handed it to Alexis. "Get your hair wet. While you wash your body, I'll wash your hair." Marta was gentle but thorough as she scrubbed Alexis's scalp and hair and then applied conditioner.

She worked quickly, using a hand-held shower nozzle to rinse Alexis's hair. When she was done, she handed Alexis a towel and hurried toward the waxing station. While Alexis dried herself, Marta adjusted the table so it was more of a reclining chair. "I'll let you know when you need to change position. For now, just lie back and relax."

Easy for you to say, Alexis thought, but she just nodded and did as directed.

Using a pair of barber scissors, Marta clipped Alexis's pubic hair close. Then she picked up a tube of something. "I call this my no scream cream," she said with a grin as she squeezed a mound onto her palm. "It numbs the nerves on the skin so it doesn't hurt so much when the wax is removed. We'll just let it do its work while I start with your legs and underarms."

She spread the cream over Alexis's pubic mound and labia, working quickly and methodically, as professional as any lab technician, though the fact she was nearly as naked as Alexis herself, not to mention extremely beautiful, provided an interesting distraction.

Next, she turned her attention to Alexis's legs, smoothing the wax in long, even strips with a flat wooden applicator and then pressing cloth rectangles over the spot and yanking them away. It hurt, but not too much. Though Alexis was brimming with questions for the staff slave, she didn't want to distract her from her work.

The underarms were worse, and a few drops of blood appeared in her left armpit but Marta just dabbed them away without comment. "Almost done. Now for your privates. This part will hurt more, but just think of it as erotic pain, if you can. And if that doesn't work, just know you're pleasing your Master by doing this. That's all that really matters, isn't it?"

Was it? Alexis had no idea, she realized. She

wasn't even entirely sure she wanted the kind of fulltime, 24/7 servitude where you put your needs and desires entirely secondary to those of your Master, voluntary though it might be. She was sexually masochistic, yes, and believed she could be submissive to the right man in the right circumstance, but realized she wasn't entirely sure what that even meant.

Don't overanalyze, she told herself. This is why you are here—to learn and gain insight. You've been handed a trainer, free of charge. Don't look a gift Master in the mouth.

Suddenly curious, she asked Marta, "Are you owned? I mean, I get it you're a staff slave here at The Compound, but do you belong to someone in particular? How does it work here?"

Marta ducked her head shyly, a pink blush moving over her smooth dark skin. "Yes. I belong to Mistress Miriam." She smiled now, a wide, beautiful smile, the love light evident in her eyes. She glanced suddenly at the clock on the wall. "Now, no more talking. I have to get you done."

Numbing cream or no, the waxing of Alexis's most delicate parts hurt like hell, but at least Marta was relatively quick and efficient about it. When she was done, she smoothed cool aloe vera gel over the area. "It won't hurt so much next time," Marta promised. "You'll be groomed once a week, or more if necessary. You must always be completely smooth. You want to see?"

She led Alexis over to the large bank of mirrors

over the sinks. "That redness will go away in a few hours," she reassured Alexis as they both stared at her denuded body. Alexis couldn't quite decide how she felt about it. She'd thought she would look like a little girl, but in fact she looked every bit a woman, her sex pooching provocatively between her legs like a flower waiting to bud.

After a few seconds, Marta said, "You can admire yourself later. Let's get your hair and makeup going. She pointed to a stool and Alexis sat dutifully, letting Marta blow dry and brush her long, thick hair into a shiny, silken curtain around her face and down her back.

"Turn toward me so I can do your makeup," Marta instructed. Alexis rarely wore much makeup, and was a little apprehensive as Marta brushed and sponged various liquids and powders onto her face. But when she turned back to the mirror, she was both startled and pleased by the results. Her skin looked dewy and luminescent, her eyes large and sparkling, her lips like the softest crushed rose petals.

"Three minutes to spare," Marta said triumphantly. "Come on. I'll show you your room." She led Alexis out of the bathroom and down the hall to the third door on the right, which was ajar. Inside Alexis saw that her clothing had been neatly piled on top of the small bureau, her suitcase resting beside it. The mattress was narrow but the duvet looked soft and clean, with a plump pillow at the head of the bed. On the wall above it hung a red nylon dog leash and a black riding crop.

"You saw how I was kneeling when you entered the bathroom?" Marta asked, drawing her attention away from the implements on the wall. Alexis nodded. Marta pointed to the throw rug on the wooden floor beside the bed. "Kneel there in that position. It's called the at-ease position. Face the open door." She watched as Alexis complied.

"Back straighter." Leaning down, Marta placed her hand on Alexis's shoulder. "Spread your thighs more. Master John will want to have a good view of your smooth cunt." This was said matter-of-factly as Marta tapped at Alexis's thigh with her bare toe. "Good. Hands resting naturally on the thighs. Eyes straight ahead. Chin up." She put a

finger beneath Alexis's chin. "Better. Now stay that way. Master John said not to move." She bent down and kissed the top of Alexis's head. "Good luck!" And she was gone.

Alexis's heart had slipped into a higher gear. Any second now she would hear the clicking of Master John's black boots in the hall. She drew in a breath and let it out slowly, willing herself to calm down. Her nipples were perking, her newly-bared sex twitching in anticipation of the Master's return. She clenched and unclenched her hands on her thighs as she waited in nervous anticipation of his return.

I belong to Mistress Miriam. Marta's face had blossomed with pure happiness when she'd said that. Were they lovers? Though Alexis considered herself primarily straight, she had enjoyed the occasional sexual romp with a girlfriend, though it had been years since those wine-soaked sleepovers.

She thought about the way Mistress Miriam had touched her after the caning, bringing her to an intense orgasm. She could easily imagine falling in love with the regal, beautiful Domme, if you were hardwired that way.

Her thoughts drifted then to Master Paul and she sighed. Probably it was for the best she hadn't been assigned to him. She wasn't at all attracted to the handsome but cold Master John, and that was all to the good. She could focus on her training and submission, without her emotions getting scrambled into the mix.

Where is he? It's been at least ten minutes, maybe longer.

Alexis shifted on the throw rug, her knees a little sore. She glanced down at her bare body and spread her thighs for a better view of her denuded pussy. Her labia were a deep pink, still shiny from the aloe vera gel Marta had smoothed over her. She touched the delicate folds and moved her hand over her sex, enjoying the smooth, soft feel of her skin.

Master Paul entered her mind's eye again, as he'd been in the swimming pool, a golden god, his tan body sparkling wetly in the sunlight as he tossed his long hair from his face. Without quite realizing what she was doing, Alexis slipped her fingers into her pussy, feeling the suck of her vaginal muscles as she imagined Master Paul, naked as he rose over her on strong arms. She closed her eyes, almost feeling the insistent nudge of his hard cock as he pressed inside her.

She wrapped her other arm around herself, feeling his warm embrace as he pulled her close. You belong to me, Alexis. I own you. His tawny golden eyes are filled with love, and also a dominant power that thrills her to her bones. She knows the lovemaking is just the preamble to the long, intense whipping he will give her afterwards, and then he will take her again into his bed and make love to her until she is gasping, begging him to stop, to never stop, oh please, oh god, oh —

Alexis gave a startled cry as she was jerked upright by a handful of her hair. "What the hell do you think you're doing!" Master John's voice was hard and angry, his face dark with fury. Still using her hair, he threw her onto the bed, face down.

Stunned and humiliated, Alexis stammered, "Oh god, I'm sorry! I'm sorry, I didn't mean to. I—"

"You didn't mean to jerk yourself off when I'd given you express orders to wait in position for me? How dare you touch that body without permission? Didn't you read the contract? Don't you understand your position here?" He gave a snort of disgust. "I can see I have my work cut out for me with you."

Alexis felt a hard hand on her lower back holding her in place as the other hand came crashing down with a furious thwack on her ass. She grunted in pain and surprise.

"You," he said, his stinging palm landing again

on her ass, "are" — thwack — "a" — thwack — "disobedient" — thwack — "little slut" — thwack — "and" — thwack — "must

be" — thwack — "punished."

He smacked her harder than she'd ever been smacked in the playful spanking scenes she'd enjoyed in the past. There was nothing playful about this spanking. It was a beating, pure and simple.

She began to struggle against him, the pain too much to handle. "Please," she begged, crying, "I'm sorry! I'm sorry! Please, you're hurting me!" Unable to control herself, she reached back, trying to cover her bruised, stinging bottom with her hands. He swatted them angrily away and then grabbed them, pulling her arms up over her head and gripping her wrists tightly.

He continued to spank her, each blow as hard as the last, until all the fight went out of her and she lay limp and whimpering. Finally he stopped, but only to drag her from the bed. He forced her onto the floor, pushing her head down onto his foot.

"Kiss my boot and thank me for your punishment, slut," he said in a tight, angry voice.

Still whimpering, Alexis touched her lips to the man's boot. "Thank you, Sir," she managed, hating him more than she'd ever hated anyone in her life.

She felt him lifting her up. "You're welcome, Alexis." The anger was completely gone from his voice and a hint of a smile moved over his face. "Now, we'll try this again. Assume a kneeling, at-ease position.

Don't move a muscle. I'll be back in a few moments."

He watched her as she eased her smarting, aching bottom carefully onto her heels. Spreading her thighs as Marta had showed her, she set her hands on her thighs and lifted her chin, unable to help sniffling.

Master John left the room, leaving her to collect herself. Her nose was running but she didn't wipe it, not daring to move after what had just happened. Jesus, talk about a bad start! Was it possible to be thrown out of the program before she even started?

She realized it wasn't Master John she hated — he'd just been doing his job. It was herself she was mad at. Silently she vowed to do better.

This time she heard the click of Master John's boots outside in the hall. When he entered, she kept her eyes forward, her chin raised, wondering if he could hear the pounding of her heart.

She felt his eyes on her, those blue, unblinking eyes. "Better," he said. He moved past her in the small space and sat on the bed. "Remaining on your knees, turn and face me," he commanded.

She twisted on the rug to face him, aware she had none of the grace Marta exhibited. "Each time I find it necessary to punish you, I will do so, but then it's over," he said calmly. "We start fresh and all is forgiven." Reaching into his black jeans, Master John pulled out a tissue and leaned down, gently wiping her eyes and nose with it, his expression almost kind.

"Thank you, Sir," Alexis said, her voice coming

out as a whisper.

He nodded curtly. "I've read your questionnaire and essays, and I believe I have some insight into what you're looking for. My methods are exacting but effective. In order to reach your true submissive core, we must break you down, tear away a lifetime of ego and self-centered gratification." He paused, looking pointedly at her, though he made no direct mention of having caught her masturbating, for which she was silently grateful.

"You will find my methods difficult at times, but I won't take you further than you're able to go. I won't give you more than you can handle. I will push your boundaries, make no mistake about that. But you need pushing — that's quite clear. You are an attractive and clearly willful woman who is no doubt used to manipulating men to get what you want, or what you think you want. That won't work with me. If I believe you're being at all flirtatious or coy, or worse, dishonest in your reactions, your punishment will be swift and unrelenting."

He let this ominous declaration sink in a moment before continuing, "By the same token, if I believe you are sincerely trying, I can promise to help you move past the barriers you've erected in your life to keep you from achieving your true submissive potential. We only have a month. That isn't a lot of time, but the good news is you will be mine 24/7, and if your training goes according to my plans, you'll be well on your way to becoming a proper sexual submissive or slave, depending what your ultimate goal is in all this."

"Please, may I ask a question, Sir?"

He nodded. "You may."

"I'm not really clear on the difference between a sexual submissive and a slave."

"In a nutshell, a sub can slip in and out of their role, depending on the situation. You give your permission each time you submit to your Dom, and he respects the hard limits you've set in advance. You will serve that Dom with the same grace and obedience as a fulltime 24/7 slave, but the relationship is less restrictive. I imagine that sort of setup is more what you're familiar with. And while rewarding, from what I've read about you, you're looking for more."

Am I? Alexis wondered, but she didn't contradict him.

Master John continued, "While you're here at The Compound, you will function as a 24/7 slave. You are my property for the duration, and you will do what I say, to the letter, regardless of your feelings on the matter. You have no rights, though you can earn privileges. You will submit to me and to anyone I choose. Ours is a somewhat artificial relationship, in that I'm your trainer rather than your actual Master. Nonetheless, I take my responsibility to you seriously, and as such I will hold you to the exacting standards I would expect of my own personal slave. Does that answer your question?"

"Yes, Master John." *My knees are killing me. I*

have to pee. Why didn't I pee when I was alone with Marta? Can I get up now? When's lunch? I'm starving.

"Now stand up. I want to inspect you."

Alexis stood, trying to mimic the fluid way Marta had risen to her feet, doubting she'd pulled it off. "Hands behind your head, fingers laced together, at attention. That's position number one, by the way. You'll get daily lessons in the positions we use here at The Compound. You will be expected to assume and hold whatever position is commanded of you, promptly and accurately."

Alexis stood as directed, memorizing the two positions she now knew — the at-ease kneeling position, and this at-attention position, also called position number one. Master John stood so they were face-to-face in the small space. He cupped her breasts in his hands, lifting and letting them fall. He tweaked her nipples, twisting and tugging at them until they stood engorged and erect. He ran his fingers along her smooth underarms. Alexis tried, and failed, to stay still as his hands moved down her sides, tickling her.

A sudden, sharp slap to her face made her gasp in surprise and shock. "You will stand absolutely still when you are inspected."

"But it tickled."

He raised his hand to silence her. "Absolutely still," he repeated. "No matter what."

Alexis pressed her lips together, her cheek stinging from the slap. Master John moved his hand again down her sides, his fingers fluttering over her skin like feathers. Somehow this time she managed to stay still. His hands moved over her stomach and down between her legs. He tapped sharply at her inner thigh. "Wider."

She obeyed, spreading her legs. He crouched in front of her, his face close to her crotch. She could feel the heat flaming in her face as he prodded and poked her bare pussy, his breath warm against her skin. His fingers moved past her cunt to her asshole, rimming the puckered entrance and then pushing inside. Though no virgin to anal play, Alexis was tense during this exam, which felt so clinical and cold, and she stiffened.

"You resist me." It was a statement and she couldn't really deny it. "That will change. You will hold nothing back from me. Nothing. I will lay you bare in every possible sense of the word. I will own you, mind, body and soul, before this month is out."

Alexis thought about this. How would she be able to give of herself to this cold, demanding man? What if she couldn't do it?

Finally Master John released her and stood. Reaching into his pocket, he pulled out a red nylon collar with an O ring at the center. "Someday you may be collared by a man who finds you worthy to be his slave. But that day is in the future. This is a training collar, used primarily for my convenience and to remind you of your place. You will remove it to shower, and at no other time while you serve me. Lift your hair."

Alexis untwined her fingers and lifted the hair from the back of her neck, dipping her head forward as Master John buckled the stiff collar around her neck. Once it was secured, he reached for the leash and clipped it onto her collar.

"Come," he said, pulling her from the room. She stumbled at first and had to walk quickly to keep up with his long stride. They were moving again down the hall toward the bathroom. Alexis was half expecting to see Marta inside, kneeling placidly on the mat beside the bathtub, but when they entered, the large room was empty.

Master John dropped the leash and moved toward the sinks. He washed his hands vigorously and then dried them on a hand towel before turning to her.

"Do you need to use the facilities before we go to lunch?"

Lunch! Yay!

"Yes, Sir." She glanced uncertainly at the row of toilets.

"Go on," he said. "You have permission. Remember, you are never, ever to use the toilet without my express permission. That is my body. You may, however, ask when you need to go, and I will decide whether to let you or not. Do you understand?"

"Yes, Master John." *Is this really happening? Did I really sign up for this? Have faith in the process,* she reminded herself. *Trust that this man knows what the hell he's doing.*

She hesitated a moment, wondering if he was just going to stand there, watching her with those unblinking owl eyes while she peed. Apparently, he was going to do just that. Biting back a sigh, Alexis moved toward the first toilet and sat, looking away as she willed her body to relax enough to pee. Finally she managed, feeling relief as her full bladder emptied. She wiped herself and flushed, and moved to the bank of sinks to wash up. She glanced at herself in the mirror, surprised but pleased to see her makeup and mascara were still intact after the spanking and her crying. That Marta was something, all right.

Master John led her out of the building and back toward the main house, though this time they entered through a back door. She felt silly being led along on a leash, though she figured she'd get used to it soon enough. He led her into a large dining room. There were easily a dozen people at the table, and lunch appeared to be in full swing. Everyone turned to look at her as they entered the room, but after a moment they resumed their eating and conversation.

She realized there were other naked and nearly naked people at the table, though they weren't on the chairs. Rather, they were kneeling or sitting cross-legged on cushions set just beside each chair at the long table. She saw Marta kneeling beside

Mistress Miriam, gazing adoringly at her as she spooned something into the slave's mouth. Alexis saw Josh a few seats down being fed by a man in his forties with salt and pepper hair.

Master John led her to an empty seat on the far

side of the table and pointed to the cushion beside it. Alexis settled herself there, watching hungrily as Master John heaped what looked like linguini onto his plate, along with a fat piece of grilled salmon and some green peas. Ignoring her, he tucked into the food, taking several bites before pouring himself what looked like iced tea from a silver pitcher.

Alexis's stomach rumbled audibly and she swallowed the saliva that had pooled in her mouth. What about me, you bastard? she thought, aware she wasn't being very submissive or patient, but too hungry to care.

Then her eye caught the man sitting just across from Master John. Master Paul. "Oh," she said softly, before realizing she'd spoken aloud. Master John was holding out a fork twirled with pasta and she leaned up, opening her mouth like a baby bird. It was delicious, covered in melted butter and tangy parmesan cheese.

When Master John was occupied again with his plate, Alexis stole another look at Master Paul, his coppery hair dry now, his face handsome in profile as he said something to the person sitting to his right. Then Master Paul straightened. He gazed directly at Alexis, those unusual tawny eyes looking directly into her soul.

"Alexis," snapped Master John. "Eyes on me." He held out a forkful of salmon. Alexis chewed, not tasting it. When she could look again, Master Paul had turned away. He was leaning down toward the lucky person kneeling naked beside him, obscured from

Alexis's view by the linen tablecloth between them. Whoever the girl was, Alexis hated her instantly.

Mine, she thought, though she knew it was ridiculous. He should be mine.

Chapter 3

After lunch, Alexis was led from the dining room and up two flights of stairs. What she could see of the second floor as they passed consisted of bedrooms, which she guessed might be occupied by Mistress Miriam and the trainers who lived on the grounds.

The third floor had been converted into one huge room, and turned out to be a fully equipped BDSM dungeon with all the familiar restraining devices and torture implements Alexis recognized from the various clubs she'd frequented over the years, as well as additional items she had never seen before but which looked diabolically intriguing.

Several other trainers and their charges were already in the dungeon, and a few more pairs trickled in as Master John gave Alexis a brief tour of the facilities. She kept surreptitiously scanning the room for any sight of Master Paul, but he was nowhere to be seen. A sudden, hard jerk of her hair made Alexis cry out.

"You are not focused. That is a very negative

trait, and one you have exhibited with alarming consistency in just the little time we've spent in one another's company." Master John's voice was hard, his expression grim.

"I'm sorry, I—"

He cut her off. "Another negative trait in a slave is the habit of speaking when not asked a direct question. This may be my fault, as I haven't yet specifically outlined the rules to you. So pay attention. You will only speak in answer to a direct question, unless you are in extreme distress. If that is the case, you may ask for permission to speak, and I will decide at that time whether or not to give that permission."

What about a safeword? Alexis wondered, but she knew enough not to stoke the fires of Master John's wrath. "We need to nip your lack of focus and failure to follow basic rules in the bud. A solid paddling should get your attention in that regard."

Taking Alexis by the shoulders, he propelled her toward a whipping post. "Sam, assist me," he called as he pushed her along. Alexis saw he was addressing a man of medium height with massive shoulders and a barrel chest who stood against the wall as erect as a military cadet. He was wearing what she now recognized as the staff slave uniform—a black thong that hugged his sizable package, and a thick black leather collar with a shiny padlock at the throat.

"Lift your arms," Master John commanded, and Alexis obeyed, her heart smacking painfully in her chest. As her wrists were locked into cuffs high over her head against

the post, she stole a glance over the large room, deeply embarrassed that she was to be punished so publicly. But no one else seemed to be paying them the slightest attention, apparently occupied with their own lessons in bondage and discipline.

The wood of the whipping post was smooth and hard against her breasts and stomach. The sudden, brutal smash of what felt like a two-by-four plank of solid wood crashed against her already tender ass, ripping a primal grunt from Alexis's mouth. Another blow landed as hard as the first, covering both ass cheeks in a burning explosion of pure, non-erotic pain. It seemed to go on and on, each blow pushing her hard against the whipping post as she whimpered and writhed in her cuffs.

"Nooooo!" she screamed finally, unable to stop herself. "Nooo! Stop! Lemon, lemonlemonlemon!"

Lemon was her safeword at the club, not that Master John knew that, but the word kept tumbling from her lips, a staccato counterpoint to the steady smashing of the wood against her poor, flaming bottom.

Finally, finally the beating stopped. Alexis sagged hard against the cuffs, her body covered with sweat, every nerve ending screaming with pain. When the cuffs were released, she sagged down the post to her knees, crying quietly.

An insistent prodding with the toe of Master

John's hard boot against her thigh made her open her eyes. "Thank me," he ordered curtly.

Not daring to disobey, Alexis dipped her head down, her tears splashing the man's boot as she forced her lips to touch it in an approximation of a kiss. "Thank you, Sir," she managed to croak.

He lifted her, gently this time, and placed his arm around her shoulders. "Can you walk?"

"Yes, Sir." Her bottom was flaming, but as the panic had ebbed, she realized it had only been a paddling. She would probably have bruises, but was otherwise intact. They moved together toward a far corner of the dungeon.

Master John directed Alexis onto a wooden platform that was raised about a foot off the ground. "Position two," he said, pushing on her shoulder.

Alexis tried to recall position two. She knew position one — standing at attention, hands behind her head. The only other position she'd been shown was the kneeling at- ease position. That had to be position two. She sank to her knees, her muscles straining a little as she held her sore, throbbing ass just above her heels. She spread her thighs wider to maintain her equilibrium and looked at Master John through her tears.

"Tell me why you were punished." For the second time that day, he produced a tissue and wiped her tears.

She swallowed, trying to think of what it was he

wanted her to say. "Because I'm not focused."

He nodded. "What else?"

"Because I spoke without being asked a direct question."

"That's correct. I have to say, I'm rather surprised. Most trainees have at least some modicum of basic protocol when they enter the program."

Alexis felt her face burning. "Permission to speak, Sir?"

"Go on."

"I'm really sorry I keep fucking up. I'm not used to this—this level of intensity. You're very rough with me. No disrespect, Sir, but if I was perfect already, I wouldn't need the training. Everything's going so fast. I can't seem to get my bearings. I guess I didn't really understand what I was getting myself into."

Master John lifted his eyebrows. "Getting yourself into? Are you saying you'd like to get yourself out? That can certainly be arranged. This isn't a prison. Your stay here is completely voluntary."

"No!" Alexis burst out, surprising herself at the vehemence of her response. "No, please. I'm sorry. I want to stay. I need to be here." She realized as she said this it was true. She had been searching her entire adult life for something just beyond her grasp. She'd been given an amazing opportunity to go deeper in her exploration than she ever could on her own. Don't blow it, Alexis. Not now. "I know I have a long way to go, Master John. Please don't give up on me."

She bit her lip, unsure what his reaction would be. To her relief, he smiled. "I appreciate your honesty. I admit I'm used to working with subs with more basic training under their belts. Maybe we need to slow down just a little. You will stay there on the punishment platform for the rest of the afternoon session. You can watch and listen as the other trainers work with their subs. Pay attention. Maybe you'll actually learn something." He was still smiling.

Alexis nodded gratefully. "Yes, Sir. Thank you, Sir."

Master John looked toward Sam, who was standing beside the platform, his arms folded over his massive chest, his expression neutral. "Keep an eye on her. Conversation is permitted. She is not to move from the platform, though she may change position if necessary."

"Yes, Master John," Sam replied.

After Master John left the dungeon, Alexis stayed quiet for a while, thinking about the whirlwind of events since she'd arrived at The Compound earlier that morning. Could she have fucked up any worse? She was lucky Master John was patient, she decided. It was humiliating to be left here on the punishment platform with a staff slave to watch over her, but at least Master John was giving her another chance.

She would do what he said and watch the scenes going on around her. She would try, as he'd suggested, to learn something. They were similar to the scenes that were played out at the BDSM clubs, except that these were more intense—more real. Even the atmosphere of the dungeon itself was different—instead of the dark walls and dim lighting of the basement BDSM clubs she was used to, the space was filled with natural light from skylights overhead, the walls painted a peaceful pale blue. There were no

groups of gawking, horny men using the scenes as fodder for later masturbation. These were serious-minded folk there to train and learn, not just to get their rocks off.

Shifting a little in an effort to get more comfortable, Alexis watched a naked young woman several yards away who stood ramrod straight, a book balanced on the top of her head while her trainer, a wiry man of about forty with thick salt and pepper hair and the requisite uniform of all black, snapped a long, cracking bullwhip against her body. Somehow the girl managed to remain perfectly still, the book never shifting on her head, though Alexis could see from her wincing expression that the bullwhip was hitting the mark.

Several yards on the other side there was a guy so trussed up with rope only his erect cock and heavy balls were visible. His arms and legs were fully extended, creating a human X, secured by still more rope to thick metal hooks in the ceiling and floor. A hood had been placed over his head, and a female trainer was touching the tip of a red shock prod to his exposed genitals. Each time it made contact, the man's body jerked and a muffled cry was heard from beneath the leather hood.

Alexis watched an older woman on her knees in front of a young male slave, his huge cock thrusting into her open mouth as a trainer stood behind her with a single tail, snapping it against her ass and back as he urged, "Focus!"

In spite of her sore bottom, Alexis felt her sex moistening and swelling as she took in the intense, erotic scenes all around her. She kept her hands firmly on her thighs, however. No way would she touch herself again without Master John's express direction. The thought warmed her, somehow, and something that had been wound tight inside her eased, at least a little.

"You're new, aren't you?" Sam asked from beside her.

"I guess that's kind of obvious, huh?" she replied ruefully.

He smiled kindly. "Give it a little time. This is your first day, right?" As Alexis nodded, Sam continued, "Master John is tough, even by Compound standards. He gets results though. Wendy, she's a fulltime staff slave now. When she came in for training, she was a willful slut, focused on her own pleasure with no concept of what service is."

Shit, Alexis thought. That sounds uncomfortably like me!

"A month with Master John set her to rights,"

Sam said, thankfully not privy to Alexis's thoughts. "So much so that she quit her job on the outside and petitioned to live here fulltime as his personal slave. She had to prove her worthiness through a series of public tests, but she belongs to Master John now."

"What does she do all day while he's, uh, working?"

"She works in the kitchen. She was a chef before she moved here last year." "And she's okay with his, you know, with what he does?"

Sam smiled and shrugged. "Sure she is. She belongs to him, not the other way around. They live in one of the cottages out on the back of the property that are reserved

for couples who want their privacy. She's going to take his brand soon. You ever been to a branding ceremony?"

Alexis shook her head, hugging herself at the thought of a fiery brand burning its way into her flesh. To distract herself from the image as much as anything else, she asked, "Are you owned?"

Sam shook his head. "Not in the way you mean. Not by an individual Mistress or Master. I'm a Compound slave. I belong to everyone here. Every Dominant on staff, that is. I service whoever needs or wants me. I live to serve."

Alexis glanced sharply at him, thinking for a second he was being sarcastic, but his expression was suffused with such fervent happiness that she understood he meant it. Curious, she asked, "What does that mean exactly? I mean, I see what you do here, helping out with misbehaving trainees" — she gave a self-deprecating laugh — "but how else does a Compound slave serve?"

"In whatever capacity I'm needed," he replied.

Unable to resist asking, Alexis persisted, "Sexually, too?"

"Absolutely. Whatever any Master or Mistress requires of me, I will do it without hesitation. It's what I was born for." His face had taken on a serene glow. His cock, she couldn't help noticing, was now tenting the tight thong.

"Mistresses and Masters?" she queried, the unspoken question, are you gay, balanced between them.

He grinned, nodding. "I'm one of the lucky ones. I go both ways. I love women, but men turn me on just as much. If a Master wants me to suck his cock, I'll drop to my knees and give him everything I've got. If he wants to fuck me up the ass, I'll assume position 8 and thank him when he's done."

"What's position 8?"

"It's the anal penetration position. There are two of them actually. Position 8a is when you remain standing. You bend over, grab your ankles and stick out your ass. More common is position 8b, which is kneeling, forehead touching the ground. Keeping that position, you would then reach back and spread your ass cheeks."

Alexis absorbed this a moment. "How many positions are there?"

"Ten basic positions, and then variations within each position. You'll learn them in the next few days. Make sure you do, because I know for a fact Master John is a real stickler when it comes to protocol. He's old school and totally into the rituals of BDSM training."

Sam said something else, but Alexis didn't hear him, because at that moment Master Paul entered the dungeon, leading a tall woman with cascades of curling blond hair falling down a long, slender back. A spasm of longing moved through Alexis as Master Paul held out his hand, helping the woman onto a concrete brick.

In profile to Alexis, with one foot in front of the other for balance, the woman stood tall and proud on the small block. In a graceful movement, she raised her arms over her

head, grasping each wrist with the opposite hand. Even with her perched on the block, Master Paul was still taller than the girl, and he reached for her hair, twining it into a loose knot at the nape of her neck and draping the makeshift ponytail over her shoulder.

The gesture reminded Alexis of Arthur's thoughtfulness and she missed him suddenly. He would, she knew, miss her too. They'd been favorite scene partners at the club. What would he do without her now? She smiled inwardly, aware such a capable and caring Dom would easily find other partners. But his giving her this gift of a chance to really discover herself—that went beyond play partners. It was the action of a true friend, a friend she would never forget, no matter where this training took her.

Master Paul moved behind the lovely young woman, selecting a heavy, thickly- tressed flogger from the wall, Alexis's favorite kind of whip. He started lightly, brushing the woman's back and ass with a sensual swish of leather. She remained still as a statue, a serene smile on her lovely face.

Master Paul struck her harder, putting his whole arm into the movement. Even from several yards away, Alexis could hear the compelling, erotic sound of leather against skin, and she wished it was she balanced with such grace and ease on the block. Would she ever attain that level of training and acceptance?

"Who is that with Master Paul?" Alexis finally managed to ask Sam, though she couldn't take her eyes from the flogging scene. Master Paul moved with the strength and grace of a dancer, whirling the flogger with expertise, his eyes fixed on the beautiful woman as he whipped her.

"That's Tiffany. This is her last week. I heard she's been placed with a very wealthy Master from Texas."

"Wow," Alexis said. "She's amazing."

Sam nodded. "She is that." And then, as if he

could read her mind, Sam added, "She started somewhere too, don't forget. She didn't just waltz in here and jump onto that brick all perfectly trained. You'll get there. Give yourself time. And have faith. Faith in your trainer and faith in yourself."

Alexis nodded gratefully. "Thank you," she said softly.

A second man in black, whom Alexis recognized as having sat next to Master John at lunch, approached Tiffany from the front. He, too, held a heavy flogger in his hand. He and Master Paul nodded toward each other, and the second man began to flog Tiffany on the front of her body. The leather tresses snaked over her breasts, her flat belly, her smooth mons and her thighs, while Master Paul flogged her from behind. Tiffany's skin was reddening, and Alexis thought she could make out the glimmer of sweat along her sides and on her forehead, but still the woman balanced on the concrete block as if she herself were carved from stone.

While Alexis watched, the woman's head began to fall back, her chin lifting until her face was parallel with the high dungeon ceiling. With her lips parted, her eyes

closing, her chest slowly rising and falling, it looked as if she were in a deep sleep as the men continued to flog her.

"She's flying," whispered Sam rapturously.

"Oh," Alexis murmured, mesmerized. The concept of moving past erotic pain into such unfettered, liberated euphoria was certainly familiar to Alexis as a player in the BDSM scene, but she'd never even come close to experiencing it for herself. Nor, she realized now as she watched, had she ever witnessed it, not this degree of intensity and grace.

"Oh," she said again, every part of her aching with longing for the experience she was witnessing. Was Sam right? Could she ever get to such a state of pure grace?

By some silent agreement the two men dropped their floggers, each moving close to Tiffany, who leaned back against Master Paul, her arms folding inward against her chest. Bending down, he scooped the naked woman into his arms and carried her toward a low couch not far from where Alexis perched on the punishment platform.

As if feeling her eyes on him, Master Paul chose that moment to look up, his gaze falling directly on Alexis. His mouth lifted in the hint of a smile and he cocked his head slightly, as if to say, What are you doing up there on the punishment platform, you naughty girl?

Alexis felt herself flushing and she looked down, wishing she could somehow disappear. Her eyes still on her thighs, she asked Sam quietly, "Does Master Paul have a fulltime slave?"

Sam replied teasingly, "Why, are you in the market for the position?"

Alexis's flush deepened. "What? No! I'm here to

learn. It's just—he's so..."

Sam laughed kindly. "I'm teasing you. To answer your question, no, he doesn't have a personal slave. Not yet, anyway."

Sam suddenly stood at attention, his arms stiff at his sides, his chin lifting. Alexis followed his gaze. Master John had returned and was striding toward them. Alexis took a deep breath and straightened her back, lowering her gaze submissively as her trainer approached.

Alexis forced the lingering image of Master Paul from her mind. She was not there to be distracted by some guy, no matter how sexy or good looking he might be. She was there to explore her submissive potential. She was there to learn from the trainer she'd been assigned to. And that, she promised herself resolutely, was exactly what she would do.

Chapter 4

The dungeon had begun to clear. Even Master Paul and his lovely slave girl had gone and within a minute or so the place was empty. "Sam, I know it's free time now, but can you stay with us for a while longer?" Master John said.

"Of course, Sir. It would be my privilege," Sam replied.

Master John helped Alexis from the punishment platform. Her legs had stiffened from so much time in the same kneeling position, and her right thigh cramped painfully as she stood.

"You'll get used to staying in positions for longer and longer periods of time," Master John said, noting her discomfort. "We have daily stretch and toning classes, along with the positions work. For now, just do a bit of stretching on your own. Then we're going to engage in an exercise with Sam's help."

After Alexis stretched her leg muscles and shook out the kinks, Master John led her to one of the many yoga pads that were scattered at intervals throughout the dungeon space, Sam following behind.

Pointing, Master John said to Alexis, "Kneel upright, knees forward, shoulders back, hands clasped behind your back."

She did as she was told, wondering what he had planned. He had Sam stand in front of her. "Remove your thong, Sam."

Without a trace of self-consciousness, Sam stepped out of the spandex thong and kicked it aside. His cock, even semi-erect, was perhaps the largest Alexis had ever seen, hanging several inches past his plum-shaped balls. He, too, was waxed smooth as a baby.

"An important trait in a trained sub is the ability to be fully in the moment," Master John said as he retrieved a nearby stool and placed it beside Alexis and Sam. He sat down on it. "Anticipation, while useful perhaps if you're trying to intuit another's needs, has no place in a service sub's repertoire. Your sole goal is to obey what is asked of you."

Alexis nodded, though in fact she was already anticipating what this exercise, as he'd called it, would be. He wanted to see how accomplished a cocksucker she was. She assessed Sam's already rising cock and swallowed, hoping she was up to the task.

"Keep your hands behind your back. Make Sam hard with your mouth."

Alexis leaned forward, wrapping her lips around the fat head of Sam's sizable cock. She sucked as much of the long, thick shaft into her mouth as she could. As it lengthened and hardened, she stroked the underside with her tongue and glided her lips farther down the shaft, attempting to take the whole of it into her mouth and down her throat, no easy feat.

A sudden, sharp tug of Alexis's hair jerked her back, and Sam's cock fell from her lips.

"You need to listen," Master John hissed, his voice tight.

"But—" Alexis began defensively, before clamping her mouth closed. She hadn't

been asked a direct question. But what had she done wrong? Why was he angry?

As if reading her mind, Master John said, not to her, but to Sam, "What did she do wrong, Sam?"

"She did more than you directed. You said to make me hard. She was already working to suck me off."

"That's correct. In a word—she anticipated." He let go of Alexis's hair. "We'll try again. Alexis, place your mouth over the head of Sam's cock. You may stroke just the head with your tongue."

Embarrassed, Alexis leaned forward again, this time determined to follow his command to the letter. She caught Sam's cock with her lips and wrapped them again around the head. She swiveled her tongue over the smooth skin and along the slit at its center. She wanted to take him more fully into her mouth. She wanted to reach for those plum balls with one hand

and wrap her other around the base. She wanted to show them both how accomplished she was at cocksucking.

She resisted, continuing only to move her lips and tongue over and around the head of Sam's cock for what seemed like a very long time. Finally, Master John said, "Take the full length of him into your throat."

Ah, at last. Eagerly she leaned forward, doing her best to accommodate the incredibly well-endowed man. She willed her throat muscles to relax, determined to demonstrate her skill. Sam groaned softly as she massaged his shaft with her throat muscles and tongue. She pulled back a little to increase the pressure and sensation and then bobbed forward again, this time taking a little more than she'd been able to a moment before.

Again she felt the sudden, fierce tug as Master John wrapped his fingers in her hair and jerked her, even harder than before, from her task. Unable to stop herself, Alexis gave a cry of dismay as Sam's glistening cock fell from her lips.

"Ego," Master John intoned, his fingers still entwined painfully in Alexis's hair, "has no place in a slave's repertoire either. You seek to impress, and you continue to anticipate. Now, let's try again. Take Sam's cock into your throat. Do nothing else. Just that." He let her hair go.

Tears pricking her eyelids, Alexis again took Sam's cock into her mouth, moving slowly forward to take his length. She was tense but too frustrated and upset to relax.

When the head of his cock moved past her soft palate and touched the back of her throat, she gagged. Instinctively she started to pull back, but stopped herself in time.

Get it right this time, damn it. Don't fuck up. Relax. Relax

Closing her eyes, she willed her throat muscles to open and soften. She felt Master John's hand on the back of her head and stilled, afraid he was again going to pull her hair for some infraction. But he only gently pushed her forward, which caused Sam's cock to go even deeper. She gagged again, but Master John didn't let go. Somehow she worked past the reflex, trying to breathe through her nose as Sam's cock blocked her windpipe. When Master John removed his hand, she almost reared back, but caught herself in time. He hadn't given her any command, other than the one to take Sam's cock into her throat.

Do nothing else. Just that.

Her legs were hurting again, and she clasped her hands together to keep from fidgeting. Sam's cock was heavy and thick in her mouth and throat, and saliva was pooling around it, which she was unable to swallow. Her eyes began to water and she thought she was going to gag again, but she somehow managed to will away the need. She imagined wide, deep blue skies, a single bird soaring high in the heavens. She thought of a thick, soft quilt she would lie down on, and then visualized a tub of steaming, sweetly scented water.

After hours, or at least what felt like hours, Master John finally said, "Good. Pull back and let him go. Remain in position three."

Alexis did so, sucking in a huge breath of air, relieved and thrilled she'd finally done something right. His single word of praise warmed her to her bones.

"Thank you, Sam," Master John said. "As a token of my appreciation for your services, you may ejaculate on Alexis's face and breasts. Then you may dress and go."

Wait. What?

"Yes, Sir. Thank you, Sir," Sam replied, his face splitting into a smile. Grabbing his cock, he stroked himself furiously, and within seconds he began spurting ribbons of white jism. Gobbets of the gooey stuff landed in warm splatters over her face and breasts, and Alexis squeezed her eyes and mouth shut, any lingering warmth from the trainer's praise lost in a new wave of humiliation and confusion.

Stepping back, Sam pulled on his thong, bowed respectfully in Master John's direction, and padded out of Alexis's line of vision. She brought a hand to her face, trying to wipe a blob of the sticky ejaculate from her eyelid.

"What are you doing?" Master John snapped. "Did I tell you to move out of position?"

Was he kidding? Did he really expect her to leave Sam's come dripping from her face and breasts? Apparently he did. Biting back a sigh, Alexis stopped what she was doing and put her hands again behind her back, clasping her wrists. She could feel the flame of a blush moving up her throat to her cheeks.

Master John stood, pulling her leash from his pocket. He clipped it to her collar and tugged. "Let's go. I'll take you back to the slave quarters. You have free time until dinner. You are to stay in the slave quarters. You can shower, nap, visit with the other trainees—whatever suits you. Dinner is at seven o'clock, sharp. I will expect you on my cushion at six fifty, ready and waiting."

Alexis rose, come still dripping from her face and smeared over her breasts. She followed the trainer from the room, down the two flights of stairs and out of the building. She was completely exhausted. She couldn't wait to get away from the exacting Master John. She couldn't wait to get into a shower and wash away this humiliation.

She had, she realized, a lot to learn.

~*~

Paul looked up from the novel he was reading at the tap on his open door. "Hey," he said. "What's up?"

John entered the room and Paul waved him toward the chair opposite his. When Paul had first come to The Compound a year ago, John had lived in the main house and their bedrooms had been next to each other. They were close in age, John being thirty-two to Paul's thirty, and they had become friends.

"I've got a new trainee," John said, settling into the chair, a clipboard in his hand.

"Yes, I know. Alexis, right?" In spite of himself, just saying her name made Paul's heart quicken a little. Which was odd, as she wasn't his usual physical type, with her voluptuous curves, dark hair and olive-toned skin. He'd always fallen for the willowy type, women with long, lean bodies, small breasts, pale skin and fair hair. Not to mention, he knew it wasn't a good idea to think of the trainees in a sexual way. They were short timers, here for their own purposes, not to satisfy the lusts of their trainers. While sex was certainly an important component of any submissive training equation, it wasn't about the trainer's gratification, but about the sub's goals and needs, and he tried always to remember that.

But something about that girl — the spark in her eyes when they'd first met and the questioning curve of her kissable mouth as he'd introduced himself — had skipped right past his usual defenses and lodged itself firmly under his skin. He didn't share this with John, of course. John would never approve. He was a strictly by the book trainer, and would never let his heart interfere with his head. Even when it had been plain to everyone but John that he was in love with Wendy, he'd still made her petition him formally, and run a whole gauntlet of tests before accepting her as his personal slave.

"Yeah." John looked down at the clipboard,

which Paul knew contained the vital statistics Miriam would have compiled to give the trainer a starting point. "She's probably one of the most inexperienced subs I've ever been assigned to train," John said. "She's fidgety, easily distracted and impatient. I actually found her with her hand buried in her cunt when she was supposed to be waiting for inspection. She was so caught up in getting herself off that she didn't even hear me come in."

"No way!" Paul laughed, though his mind shifted instantly to an image of Alexis caught in the throes of masturbation, her head thrown back, her cheeks flushed, her breath rasping in her throat. He shook his head to dislodge the image. "Is that why she was on the punishment platform?"

John barked a mirthless laugh. "Nope. That was for yet other infractions, though not quite as serious. She's just completely untrained. A total novice, though apparently Miriam saw something worthwhile in her." He shrugged, as if what that might be escaped him.

"Let's see the chart."

John handed it to him and Paul scanned the information.

Alexis Stewart Physical Statistics:

Female;

Age: 29;

Height: 5'5";

Weight: 122 pounds;

Orientation: Straight, some bisexual tendencies;

Disposition: Masochist with submissive leanings;

Fears/Current Limits: Inner fears about letting go, being perceived as out of control, weak;

Known Strengths: Intelligent. Sincere desire to submit. Highly sexual and orgasmic;

Known Weaknesses: Lack of experience. Limited pain tolerance. Some resistance to anal penetration;

Stated Goals: To learn to truly submit with honesty and passion. To release her stranglehold on control (her words) and find serenity;

Current Status: Unowned.

Initial Observations based on emails and interview: Derives intense pleasure from sensation of all kinds. Highly orgasmic. Once things cross into a territory that she does not find personally exciting, she tends to close down. She can be evasive when questioned. Despite her lack of previous training and her limited experience, I see true potential in this trainee. Beneath the trappings of ego and drive that allow her to maintain the control she thinks is necessary, there is a genuine submissive.

Recommendations:

Teach her the value of answering a direct question quickly and succinctly;

Test of pain tolerance level to see how she processes pain, as well as composure during the testing;

Work on focus;

Associate orgasm with erotic pain; Test reactions to sensory deprivation;

Expose her to stress-inducing situation, such as public humiliation, predicament bondage, orgasm denial;

Test reaction to severe bondage for extended periods.

Paul handed the clipboard back to John. "I see what you mean about inexperienced. What's Miriam's basis for the comments about Alexis's potential as a true sub?"

"Look at page two. The essay."

Paul flipped the page. The essay was handwritten, which was unusual in itself. Paul, who produced a scrawl at the best times, was impressed with the elegant, uniform lettering. He scanned the page and then began to read in earnest, his eyes moving over the heartfelt and almost painfully honest yearnings of a young woman clearly searching for something within herself. It was the last few paragraphs that really got his attention.

All my life I've been struggling to come to terms with what I am. I had difficulty reconciling my inherently submissive nature with my sense of self as a confident, successful woman. I was rewarded by society for the obvious academic and career successes I enjoyed, but I have come to realize I have always taken the easy route, using the shield of my outward success to hide the secret longings of my heart and soul.

When I discovered that there were other likeminded souls engaged in a similar search, I threw myself into the BDSM scene, hoping to connect on an intimate level, but somehow each new experience just left me a little lonelier than before, and still longing to connect in a way I have only dreamed of. I have come to understand that the problem does not lie in the inherent shallowness of the club scene, or the lack of empathy or connection with Doms with whom I have sought connection.

The problem lies with me.

I have spent a lifetime building a wall around my true submissive nature, brick, by brick, by brick. And now, when I have finally found the courage to face my need and embrace my longing, I find I don't have the tools. I need help to chip away at the mortar and knock down the bricks that are hiding the true submissive within.

Paul handed the clipboard back to John. "Impressive. So, what's your plan to help her get past her own defenses?"

"I like Miriam's suggestion about associating orgasm with erotic pain. We'll definitely be working on that. And predicament bondage will teach the discipline she sorely needs to learn to keep still during corporal punishment. Then of course the usual position training, oral service, all types of penetration, expanding her comfort zone for anal play."

Paul nodded, images of Alexis bound in rope and chain, her mouth and cunt stuffed with cock, her ass cherry red from a long, hard caning careened willy nilly in his brain and sent the blood rushing to his cock. He shifted in his chair, crossing his legs to hide the sudden erection. What the fuck was his problem?

"How's it going with Tiffany?" John asked, apparently done discussing his latest charge. "Is she ready for her final showing?"

"We're getting there," Paul replied, relieved to have something else on which to focus. "I've never seen anyone fly as easily as she does. It would be an ego stroke, except I know I've got very little to do with it. She's just a natural. If anything, I have to be careful with her. She has such a high pain threshold, I don't get the normal distress cues. She just wants more, more and more."

They discussed Tiffany's progress for a while, until John glanced at his watch. "Wendy is waiting for me back at the cottage. I'll see you at dinner?"

Paul nodded. "Yeah, see you then."

Just as John left, there was another tap at Paul's door. Janice stood there, petite and lovely in her thong. She dropped to her knees and touched her head to the floorboards, her pert ass high in the air.

"What is it, Janice?" Paul said, though of course he knew.

"Please, Sir. I'm here to service you, if you would allow me the honor."

One of the perks of being a trainer at The Compound was full access to all the staff slaves, even those specifically owned, if the owner gave his or her permission. Because of the loss of control that resulted from having an orgasm during training, trainers were discouraged from direct sexual interaction with their trainees, instead using staff slaves to serve as surrogates. As a result, by the end of the day, male trainers often developed what Paul had heard called "blue balls" by older generations of men.

Miriam, ever mindful of the needs of her trainers, sought to provide them with release. Janice was a dedicated cocksucker who often made the rounds before dinner to see if anyone was in need of her excellent services.

Images of the lovely Alexis still ripe in his mind, Paul said, "Yeah. That would be great." He stood and unbuttoned his jeans, tugging them, along with his underwear, down his thighs. Janice remained on her knees and crawled across the carpet, kneeling up in front of him.

A smile curled over her small rosebud of a mouth as she reached for him. He closed his eyes and placed his hands on her bare shoulders as she began to work her magic. Her mouth was like hot, wet silk gliding over his cock.

She took the length of him until her nose was at his pubic bone. She rested there, milking his cock with her throat muscles while doing something amazing with her tongue. Paul sighed his approval and then grunted as she gripped his balls tight, almost too tight, and she began to bob up and down on his shiny, rock-hard cock.

When he was about to come, he felt her fingers slipping between his ass cheeks. A digit pressed inside the puckered ring of muscle, her other hand wrapping around the base of his cock like a second mouth while she licked and suckled him in a frenzy of perfect friction.

Paul wound his fingers into her hair as his body shuddered and released its seed. She didn't miss a beat, swallowing while still sucking and kissing his shaft as if it was the only thing in the world that mattered. Finally, as his spasms eased and his fingers loosened their grip in her silky hair, she pulled back at precisely the right moment, when another flick of her tongue would have moved from pleasure to over-stimulation.

His pants still around his knees, Paul sank back into his chair. "Perfect," he murmured, his mind blissfully blank. After a moment he forced his eyes to open, looking down to see Janice ardently kissing the tops of his boots. He touched her shoulder and she looked up, an expression of pure rapture on her pixyish face.

"Thank you, Janice. That was amazing, as always."

Her smile glowed. "Thank you, Sir."

He watched her crawl to the door, her luscious ass swaying. Man, I love my job.

Chapter 5

After another sumptuous meal, Master John told Alexis to return to her quarters, as he had other business to attend to that evening. She had intended to check out the sitting room where the trainees and staff slaves sometimes hung out, but she made the mistake of lying down in her room for a bit, and the next thing she knew it was morning.

When Master John appeared at 6:30, she was standing in her room at attention, freshly showered, aflutter with nervous anticipation for her first full day of training. She managed to stay still as he moved his tickling fingers over her skin.

"Breakfast is at eight o'clock," he informed her, as she forced herself to put aside her immediate longing for a cup of strong black coffee. "I apologize for not being available last night. We'll make up for it this morning before breakfast. You'll need to learn the ten basic slave positions and their variations, so we'll start with that."

It was another glorious summer morning, the early sun warming her naked body as Master John led her back to the main house. This time he didn't take her to the dungeon, but to a room on the second floor. The room reminded her of Miss Tatum's School of Dance, where she'd gone for ballet lessons from age six to twelve. The walls were lined on two sides with mirrors, with waist-high polished wooden bars parallel to the gleaming hardwood floors.

A beautiful slave girl with very short red hair and large gray eyes was kneeling on a yoga mat next to a chair. The girl's knees spread wide, her hands resting palms up on her thighs. She wore the thick black leather collar of the other staff slaves, but instead of the square stainless steel padlock Alexis had observed, her padlock was shaped like a heart, and it appeared to be made of gold. As they entered the room, the young woman turned her eyes to Master John with a look of such pure, raw adoration that it took Alexis's breath away.

Master John pointed toward another nearby yoga mat. "Position two," he said to Alexis. Beside the mat stood a rack filled with crops, canes, paddles and floggers. Alexis knelt as ordered, assuming the same position as the slave girl who still had eyes only for Master John.

"This is Wendy," Master John said, moving toward the girl. A slight girl with a long, slender neck and a pixie-short haircut, she reminded Alexis of Audrey Hepburn in the old movies she liked to watch late at night on TV.

Master John put his hand on Wendy's head and she leaned into his hand, closing her eyes. When Sam had said that Master John owned a slave, it honestly hadn't occurred to Alexis that love would enter the equation, at least not his side of it. But as she watched Master John's expression soften as he looked down at Wendy, Alexis realized the girl's feelings were returned.

Turning to face Alexis, Master John said brusquely, "This morning we will work on positions training. It's essential that you learn the ten basic positions and their variations as quickly as possible. These are stepping stones as we move forward in your training. To keep it interesting, I'd like to test your reaction to certain sexual stimuli. But first, my slave will show you how it's done."

He indicated the large poster on the wall just over Alexis's head. "These are the basic positions. Wendy will demonstrate them for you. Pay close attention, as it'll be your turn next."

Alexis scanned the list, titled Basic Slave Positions, wondering how she'd ever remember all that.

Standing

Attention, hands behind your head, feet shoulder-width apart

At ease, hands behind your back

Kneeling

At ease. Back straight, thighs spread, palms

facing upward resting lightly on thighs

Offering. Facing away from Master/Mistress, kneel, cross wrists and stretch arms out, lean forward to place head on floor. Lift ass high

Dog – Fall to floor on all fours, head straight, eyes forward, ass thrust up, legs wide

Crawl – hands and knees, back arched, chin up, eyes down

Examine

Lie on back, hands at sides, palms facing upward, legs spread wide

Lie on back, hands at sides, legs spread wide, lift hips off floor

Sexual Usage

Lie on back, place feet flat up against ass, knees fully bent

Lie on back, knees moderately bent, reach forward to spread/offer genitals

Examine Flipside – Facedown, head turned to side, arms at sides, legs spread wide open

Corporal/Anal

Standing. Bend over and grab ankles, bring head as close to knees as possible, thrust out ass

Kneeling. On knees, forehead touching the

ground. Reach back and spread ass cheeks

Punishment – stand either flat footed or on toes, nose against the wall, wrists bound behind back. Male slaves – cock may not touch the wall

Spanking

Lie over Master's/Mistress's lap, hands and feet on the floor.

Lie over Master's/Mistress's lap, – hands clasped behind neck

Straddle Master's/Mistress's lap, facing his/her feet, hands on floor, ass raised

While Alexis watched, Master John took Wendy through each of the positions. She moved effortlessly through them, making even the most awkward positions seem easy and as graceful as a swan's glide on the water. Though she seemed perfect to Alexis, Master John corrected Wendy gently from time to time with a hand placed on the small of her back, or tapping at the inside of her thigh.

Turning finally to Alexis, Master John said, "One way to learn is by example. Wendy is highly trained, and her behavior is exemplary, even under the greatest strain. Before we get to you, watch and pay attention."

Turning back to Wendy, he said, "Fetch the vibrating wand and the single tail."

Wendy rose and moved toward the rack beside Alexis. She took a single tail whip, along with an oblong box and returned to kneel in front of her Master. He opened the box and withdrew a cordless vibrating wand. He handed it to Wendy. "Lubricate it," he said. She at once began to suck and lick the round rubber head of the wand as if it were a lover's cock.

"Good. Now use it on your cunt. You will come on command."

"Yes, Sir," the girl whispered, her large gray eyes on his face as she placed the wand's head between her legs and pressed the button at its base, causing it to whir to life. From Alexis's position, she could see the two of them in profile. In addition, their images were reflected from all angles in the mirrors that covered the walls. The single tail snapped against Wendy's left breast, leaving a white mark that quickly turned to pink and then dark red.

Again and again the lash struck Wendy's breasts while she knelt up, thighs spread, the vibrator whirring at her cunt. She remained perfectly still, her eyes fixed on her Master's face. When the lash caught a nipple, the mask slipped for just a second, a wince moving over the girl's face, but after a moment her features smoothed.

Alexis was riveted to the display, fascinated and awed in the face of Wendy's composure as Master John flicked the tail over and over, leaving a trail of angry red welts in its wake, while Wendy masturbated herself with the wand.

Finally he said, "Come for me, Wendy."

Within seconds the girl shuddered, her mouth falling open, her eyes wide and fixed on his face as she trembled in orgasm. All the while Master John continued to lash her breasts with the snapping single tail whip. Alexis's own cunt was throbbing as she watched the pair, both of whom ignored her completely.

When Wendy had stilled, Master John stepped back and pointed to his boots. Wendy flicked off the vibrator and set it down carefully beside her. Bending down, she kissed the tops of Master John's boots, while murmuring, "Thank you, Sir. Thank you. Thank you," with such ardent intensity Alexis could tell she really meant it.

Reaching for her, Master John pulled Wendy up and then wrapped her in his arms, kissing her first on the forehead and then on the lips, leaving no doubt whatsoever in Alexis's mind that these two were lovers. Watching them, she felt a painful tugging in her heart, as if someone had wrapped their fist around it.

Finally, with Wendy again kneeling on her mat, Master John turned to Alexis, all the tenderness that had been in his face a moment before replaced by the unblinking, cold expression with which she was more familiar. "Let's see if you learned anything."

As he had done with Wendy, he called out the various positions, and Alexis did her best to assume them. Standing over her, he corrected her far more often than he had Wendy, and when he was finally satisfied, Alexis was sweating, every muscle screaming.

Master John returned to his chair and sat like a king on his throne. "I want you to select a cane from the rack. Place it in between your teeth and then assume position three."

Her heart pounding, Alexis turned to the rack and reached for one of the shorter- handled canes. Placing it between her teeth like a dog holding a bone, she glanced yet again at the positions poster, and moved from the mat to her hands and knees.

"Position four. To me." Master John pointed to the ground in front of him. Alexis crawled toward him, trying to keep her back arched as she moved, her breasts swaying, the cane clenched in her teeth.

"Position 6B. Lie so your feet are in front of me."

Alexis's eyes slid to Wendy, who was kneeling at-ease beside Master John, eyes downcast, her face calm and serene. Recalling yesterday's lesson about anticipation, Alexis tried to keep the nervous butterflies fluttering in her gut at bay.

She lay on the hard floor in front of Master John and bent her knees, drawing them upward, her feet flat on the ground. She ran her tongue over the smooth rattan of the cane still clenched between her teeth as she reached forward to spread her labia.

"Legs wider," Master John said. "And lift your ass just a little. Yes. That's better." While Alexis held herself in this somewhat uncomfortable and very vulnerable position, Master John continued, "I am going to teach you to associate pleasure with pain until the two hold no separate distinction for you. While you are under my care, you will never orgasm without experiencing erotic pain at the same time. Our goal is eventually to train you to such a degree that you can come just from the pain alone."

Master John stood and moved to Alexis. Crouching beside her, he took the cane from between her lips. "Wendy is going to lick your cunt while I cane your breasts. You will not move. You will not cry out. You will not come, unless or until I give you explicit permission. Do you understand?"

"Yes, Sir," Alexis said, her voice breathless in her ears. She jerked slightly at the first soft, wet touch of Wendy's tongue between the folds of her sex. At the same time, Master John began to tap with the cane against her breasts. As Wendy licked in a swirl around Alexis's rising clit, the taps turned to stinging strokes on the tops of her breasts.

When he moved the cane to the undersides of her breasts, he hit her harder, making Alexis gasp in pain. "Silence," Master John admonished. He hit her harder. Alexis bit her lower lip and breathed hard through flared nostrils, trying to focus on the pleasure at her pussy instead of the stinging pain on her breasts.

Wendy's tongue moved with practiced ease, passing like butterfly wings over her clit, licking along the inner folds and sliding down to tease the entrance. Without realizing what she was doing, Alexis found herself arching her hips toward Wendy's sensual touch.

"I said don't move!" Master John's words were punctuated by the crashing impact of the cane against her right nipple.

Alexis screamed.

"Silence!" The left nipple received the same fiery attention. All the while, the slave at Alexis's cunt never missed a beat, licking and suckling as Alexis struggled to be still and silent. Tears slid down the sides of her face and into her hair. Her heart was thudding in her ears. Her fingers were slipping on her wet outer labia as she struggled to maintain her position and hold herself open.

The cane sliced against her breasts, every fifth stroke or so landing across her nipple. Try as she might, Alexis couldn't remain silent or still. Though her lips were pressed together in an effort to stay quiet, she could hear her own steady whimpering in her ears, and could feel the trembling in her body as the girl between her legs licked her relentlessly toward an orgasm she knew she wasn't going to be able to control.

Wendy did it. You can do it, too, she tried to tell herself, but she didn't really believe it. Yet she was certain what she'd witnessed had been real. Somehow, Wendy was able not only to come on command, but to do so while being lashed with a single tail. But Wendy was clearly a highly trained sex slave, while Alexis was only just starting out. Surely Master John couldn't hold her to the same standards. It wasn't fair!

Sam's words suddenly moved through her mind: You'll get there. Give yourself time. And have faith. Faith in your trainer and faith in yourself.

She tried. She really did, and for a while she was able to resist the onslaught of sensation engulfing her from all sides. Bit by bit, though, she felt herself losing the battle. Her breasts felt as if they'd been stung by a thousand angry bees, while at the same time an orgasm was building inside her, rising like a wave that she knew was going to crash at any second.

Don't come, don't come, don't come. Ah! Fuck! That hurts, it hurts, it hurts, it hurts. Don't come, it hurts, oh fuck, oh god, oh shit. Oooooooooooooooooh....

Despite her fervent desire and best efforts to obey Master John's commands, Alexis's body began to convulse in a powerful orgasm, and a low guttural moan

wrenched itself from her lips. All the while, the cane crashed down on Alexis's tender, flayed breasts while Wendy's warm wet tongue moved over her shuddering, spasming sex.

Finally unable to tolerate another ounce of stimulation, neither the pleasure nor the pain, Alexis fell out of position and curled in on herself, her hands flying to protect her aching breasts, her knees pulling up in a fetal position against her body. Dimly, she was aware of Master John speaking over the roar of her blood in her ears. She felt his hands gripping her beneath her arms and hauling her into an upright position.

Wendy was again kneeling on her mat, her face calm and serene, eyes downcast. Crouching in front of Alexis, Master John took her face in his hands and peered unblinkingly into her eyes. "Did you obey me, Alexis?"

Alexis tried to look away in her shame, but he held her fast. "Don't look away," he said sternly. "Answer the question."

"No, Sir. I tried to but—"

He slapped her face. "No excuses. You answer the question asked. You don't offer discussion unless it's invited."

Her cheek stinging, Alexis felt tears flooding her eyes and she blinked them back. Master John let her go and stood. "It's clear we have a lot of work to do." He glanced at his watch. Then he pointed to a corner of the room. "Position nine. Move."

Dazed, Alexis forced herself to her feet. She felt dizzy and disoriented as she walked toward the corner. Master John followed her. "You are to be punished. Tell me why."

"Because I came without permission, Sir." It was on the tip of her tongue again to offer excuses, to explain that there was no way she could have helped it, but she swallowed back the words, aware they would not be well received.

"Correct. And what else?"

"I wasn't still or silent, Sir." Again she wanted to

explain there was no way to be quiet and still when someone was slicing into your breasts with a cane while a beautiful woman was kneeling between your legs, her head buried in your cunt. But Alexis just pressed her lips together and kept her hands at her sides, resisting the urge to stroke her tender, welted breasts.

"That's right," Master John agreed, his tone grim. "You have very little control over your body and your reactions. I will work hard with you to teach you some control. Meanwhile, you will accept your punishment. Hands behind your back, nose against the wall."

Blinking back tears of humiliation, Alexis assumed the position. She heard him moving behind her, and a moment later felt Velcro cuffs being secured around her wrists and clipped together. Moving to stand beside her, Master John reached into his pocket and pulled out a penny. "You will hold this in place with your nose against the wall. If, when I return from breakfast, I find the coin on the floor, you will be beaten."

When he returns from breakfast? What about me? I'm hungry! I need coffee!

Alexis bit the inside of her cheek in her effort not to voice her protests. She leaned her head back while Master John held the penny against the wall, and then leaned forward, pressing against it with her nose. At least he hadn't told her to stand on her toes. *So see*, she told herself, *it could have been worse.*

Yeah, it could have been worse, but not by much. She had been awkward and graceless while trying to do the positions, she had squirmed and whimpered during the caning, and she had come without permission. Now she wasn't going to get breakfast. She would be left alone, nose against the wall, wrists cuffed behind her back.

She heard the two of them softly murmuring behind her, and then the quiet click of a door closing. The penny was hard against her nose, and her tender nipples brushed against the wall. She clenched and unclenched her fists beneath the cuffs and shifted restlessly from foot to foot, her stomach rumbling.

Finally she stilled, closing her eyes with a sigh. The morning had only just begun, and already she'd fucked things up. She was a billion years away from Wendy's level of training and grace. Was a month really enough to get her there? Did she have what it took in terms of endurance and the ability to control her body's reactions? Did she even want to be like Wendy? Completely controlled and mastered by another?

She thought of Wendy's utter grace as she moved. She thought of the way she'd kept her eyes open and on her Master's face while he whipped her, the vibrator whirring away at her cunt. She thought of the peaceful and serene look on her face. Then she thought of the look of pure love that had passed between the two of them.

Yes, she thought fervently. I do want that. More than anything I've ever wanted in my life.

Then the penny slipped, landing with a clink and rolling across the polished wooden floor.

Chapter 6

Alexis steeled herself as she heard the door opening behind her. She'd tried to retrieve the fallen penny, kneeling down and attempting to pick it up with her teeth. She'd actually gotten it into her mouth, but the transfer from mouth to nose proved to be impossible without the use of her hands. Giving up, she let the penny fall and remained in punishment position, nose to the wall, hoping that, at least, counted for something.

She heard the clomp of Master John's boots as he crossed the room. She didn't move. She saw him out of the corner of her eye as he bent down and picked up the penny. She felt him releasing the Velcro cuffs from her wrists and then his hand closed around the back of her neck. She shut her eyes, waiting for his reprimand.

"You may stand down. Punishment is over."

She jerked her head in his direction, blurting, "But the penny. I— "

He put two fingers to her lips, silencing her. "You will thank me properly for the punishment." He pointed to his boot.

Alexis dropped immediately to the ground, feeling weak with relief at the unexpected reprieve. She kissed the top of his boot. "Thank you, Sir," she said.

Master John stepped back. "I brought you some breakfast. Then it's time for the morning dungeon session."

Alexis started to thank him again, but remembered in time to keep quiet. She saw he'd set a tray down beside one of the yoga mats. On it was a mug of coffee and a plate containing scrambled eggs, toast and bacon. It smelled heavenly, and Alexis realized she was starving.

"Go on," he said. "You may feed yourself. You have three minutes."

Alexis moved quickly toward the mat and sat, not sure what position to assume. She glanced toward Master John for direction, but he gave none, so she knelt and then leaned a little to one side, reaching eagerly for the mug. She took a deep swallow of the strong, hot coffee and then tucked into the eggs. She felt a little self-conscious being watched by the unblinking, inscrutable Master John, and tried not to wolf down her food.

When she was done, he produced her leash and clipped it to her collar, using it to tug her to her feet. He led her first to a powder room on the same floor. Alexis hadn't moved her bowels since coming to The Compound, and her intestines gurgled painfully as she sat on the toilet, but beneath Master John's unblinking stare Alexis knew there was no way she would manage more than a pee.

"Morning session has already begun," Master John said as he led her up the stairs. As before, there were already several scenes in play. As they passed other trainers and their trainees, Alexis couldn't help looking around for Master Paul. She spied him with a woman she presumed was Tiffany, though it was hard to say for sure, as the top half of her body and her entire head was covered in what looked like black bandages. The partially mummified woman was lying on an exam table, her legs fully extended in a V above her body, the ankles tied with rope that was secured to hooks in the ceiling.

Master John took Alexis to the training station just beside Master Paul. A large metal table about the size of a large stool was set against a wall, two thick, sturdy poles jutting out from the wall on either side of it. Beside the table stood a small set of drawers.

"For your extended session today I will assess your ability to process prolonged, intense erotic pain and stimulation. I also want to see how you do with extreme bondage. Get up on the table."

Alexis was keenly aware of Master Paul nearby, his coppery auburn hair obscuring his face as he leaned over his charge. Stop it, she ordered herself. Focus on your trainer. She hoisted herself onto the table, her heart already thumping with anxious anticipation at the promise of intense erotic pain and extreme bondage.

"Lean against the wall so your shoulders and the back of your head are resting comfortably. Keep your ass on the front edge of the table and grab the poles on either side. Once I bind your hands, I'll take your legs, one at a time, and tie them at the ankle to the end of each pole."

Alexis reached up for the poles on either side of her as directed, wrapping her fingers around the cold metal. She watched as Master John wound rope around each wrist and knotted it into place. He appeared totally focused on his task, his lips slightly pursed as he worked. When he was done, her arms were raised on either side of her, slightly bent at the elbows. The position wasn't uncomfortable — yet.

"Now your feet." Taking one leg, Master John pulled it upward and out. He wrapped the soft, thick rope around her ankle, lashing it to the pole, and then repeated the process with her other leg. When he was done, she was completely immobilized by the ropes binding her wrists and ankles and forcing her legs wide apart.

Usually the feel of rope against her skin both aroused and calmed Alexis, but in this extremely vulnerable position she was anything but relaxed. She could hear Master Paul murmuring nearby and resisted the impulse to look his way.

Master John left her line of vision for a minute, and returned pulling a latex glove over his right hand. He squirted lubricant directly onto the fingers of the glove and then pressed a gloved finger into Alexis's ass.

Reflexively she turned her head away, closing her eyes.

"Look at me. Keep your eyes open and on my face at all times," Master John commanded. Alexis forced herself to obey, her face hot with embarrassment. Master John swiveled his finger inside of her and pressed a second digit in as well. "I sense your resistance during ass play. A properly trained slave has no modesty with her Master. We'll exploit this evident hesitation on your part and eliminate it."

He moved his fingers inside her ass and it took everything Alexis had to keep her eyes on his face as he probed and prodded her. Finally he took his fingers from her. Stripping off the glove, he bent down and opened a drawer. He lifted something into her line of vision, and Alexis saw it was an anal plug made of clear plastic. She bit her lip with trepidation but managed to stay quiet.

Though she had occasionally had anal sex in the privacy of her bedroom with a single partner, Alexis had an aversion to foreign objects being placed inside her ass, and this public setting made it all the more uncomfortable for her. She hadn't listed this as a hard limit on her application to The Compound, intellectually aware it was something she would need to work through if she was to truly submit.

She jerked as the lubricated tip of the plug made contact with her anus. Master John pushed the plug into her, his movements slow and careful. Though she couldn't tense her sphincter muscles in the position she was in, Alexis felt the tension in the rest of her body, and in the clench of her hands around the cold metal bars.

Master John must have felt it too, because he urged, "Relax. Take deep, slow breaths. Accept what I give you."

The plug felt hard and huge as it pushed its way inside her. She couldn't help the yelp of pain as the flared bottom slid home. "There," Master John said. "Make sure that stays in place during this exercise."

Bending down, he pulled a short, thin cane from the drawers and whipped it in the air in front of her. He set the cane beside her and leaned down again, this time taking out a pair of clover clamps. "You know what these are, of course," he said.

Alexis nodded, her nipples already perking. What is it about a masochist, she wondered, that we crave the pain even as we fear it? It wasn't that it didn't hurt. It was that it hurt so good.

Standing between her widespread legs, Master John leaned forward and reached for her right nipple. He twisted and pulled it until it was engorged and throbbing, and then pressed the clamp open on either side of the distended nipple. He let the rounded tips close, causing a burst of pain to zing from her nipple to her brain and then down to her clit. He did the same with her left nipple, and then lifted the chain, giving it a painful tug.

"I don't want a lot of yelping and whining. This will help you to keep quiet." He pushed the chain between her lips. "Don't let it fall. If you do, you will be punished."

Alexis took the chain between her teeth and bit down. He hadn't even begun the main part of the torture and already she felt the fear sweat pricking beneath her arms and at the small of her back.

Stepping back, Master John picked up the cane. He began to tap her inner thighs with light, stinging strokes. The cane moved down, tapping the backs of her calves. Though the cane stung, along with the humiliation of being bound as she was with a butt plug up her ass, Alexis managed to stay quiet and reasonably composed. Maybe to the casual onlooker she appeared as serene as Tiffany or Wendy, even if it took every ounce of self control to stay quiet and still.

I can do this, she told herself. I can do this. Breathe deep. Stay focused. Please Master John.

When he struck the sensitive soles of her feet, some of Alexis's composure slipped. Grunting to keep from crying out, she bit down harder on the chain in her mouth. She had never been hit on the bottom of her feet before, and the pain was intense. The thin, whipping cane cut into the tender arch of first her left foot, then her right, and back again. Unable to control herself, Alexis began writhing on the table, but she could barely move, lashed securely as she was by both wrists and ankles to the poles.

"Uncurl your toes." A painful smack of the cane to her toes made Alexis cry out, the clover clamp chain slipping from her mouth.

Bending forward, Master John picked up the chain and gave a vicious tug. Though Alexis's nipples had numbed from the compression, that jerk of the chain re-awoke the tortured nerve endings in her tender nipples, and she screamed again. Master John shoved the chain into her open mouth.

"Compose yourself," he ordered.

She bit on the chain, tears in her eyes, her chest heaving. I can't do this, she thought wildly, pleading with her eyes.

As if he could hear her thoughts, Master John said calmly, "You can do this, Alexis. You need to let go. Stop anticipating. Stop holding on to the pain. Let it go. Flow with it. Give in to it."

How often had Arthur said those exact words to her? Damn it, if she knew how to, she would!

Mercifully, Master John shifted his focus from her tortured soles. The cane whipped over her body, each stroke harder than the last. After an especially brutal stroke Alexis again dropped the chain.

"I can't," she groaned, the chain again falling from her mouth. "I can't."

"You can," Master John replied, the rattan like fire searing her already tortured, welted flesh. "Give in. Let go." Again he picked up the chain and placed it in her mouth.

Alexis felt herself edging into panic. She was clutching the poles, which were slick beneath her sweating palms. Master John's usually impassive expression clouded, a frown pulling down the corners of his mouth. Setting down the cane, he moved between her legs and leaned forward. He reached for the clamps compressing her nipples. "I'm going to take these off."

Alexis began to tremble. She turned her head away, closing her eyes, whimpering in fearful anticipation. When the clamps were released, for a fraction of a second, she felt nothing. As the blood flow returned, pain shot through her nipples and she couldn't stop herself—she opened her mouth and screamed.

Slowly she opened her eyes again, her face still to the side. As the room came into focus, she saw Master Paul looking at her. He had seen her untrained, ungraceful display. He probably was counting himself lucky he hadn't been assigned to her. Tears of shame welled in her eyes, and yet she found she couldn't look away from Master Paul's intense gaze.

"You can do it."

Alexis stilled. Master Paul hadn't spoken aloud; he had only mouthed the words, but they were clearly directed toward her. She blinked away her tears. Had she just imagined that?

Master Paul smiled, a slow, easy lift of his lips, his eyes warm and kind. Something that had been clenched too tightly inside Alexis eased at that moment, and the panic slid away.

I can do it.

This time when Master John picked up the cane, though the strokes stung just as much as a moment before, Alexis found herself better able to tolerate it. Master Paul had turned his attentions back to Tiffany, and Alexis suddenly remembered Master John's instruction to keep her eyes on his face. She turned back to her trainer, but though she might have appeared to be looking directly at him, it was Master Paul she saw in her mind's eye, with his warm, encouraging smile, mouthing the words, you can do it, over and over again as the cane came crashing relentlessly down.

"Much, much better," Master John said finally. He moved again to stand between Alexis's legs, this time reaching for the anal plug, which he pulled slowly from her ass. When it popped out, he set it somewhere out of her line of vision. She was expecting him to release her at last from the confining rope, but instead he ran his fingers lightly over her spread labia, and then pressed his fingers into her pussy.

He offered a knowing smile. "There, you see?" he said. "You're soaking wet. Through all the crying and protest, your cunt doesn't lie, sub girl." He rubbed slowly over her labia, the friction tugging indirectly at her clit. While continuing to stroke her, he slid his finger again inside, crooking it just so, making Alexis gasp at the hot, sudden rush of sensation.

"Oh," she breathed, the word pulled from her. After the searing cut of the cane, his touch was especially powerful. Pleasure radiated through her, mingling with the pain. Her cunt was throbbing, her breath coming in short gasps as she struggled to resist the rising urge to climax. His finger still inside her, he ground his palm against her clit. She was going to come. There was no way she could help it.

Again reading her mind, or maybe just reading her body, Master John said, "Remember, pleasure and pain must be combined. I want you to come, Alexis, but not from my touch. You will come from the cane."

His hand was withdrawn, replaced by the steady, rat-a-tat tapping of the cane against her swollen, aching cunt. It was light at first, more of a tease than anything, a swish of pleasure with just a hint of sting. But as he continued, the pressure increased, the pain rising to obscure the sensual stroke.

Alexis felt the sweat again at her armpits, and the tremble of her aching, taut muscles. And yet, in spite of the stinging pain at her cunt, or perhaps partially because of it, the climax that had threatened a moment before from the pure pleasure of his touch rose again, as strong or perhaps stronger than before.

Alexis clenched her teeth to keep from screaming, her poor, stinging clit throbbing with each whippy stroke of the cane against the tender flesh. "Oh god," she finally groaned, gripping the metal poles with all her strength. "Oh, please. Oh, Sir. Oh..."

"That's it. Come for me. Give of yourself completely. Hold nothing back."

Alexis's body began to buck and shudder, and

still the cane whipped down on her spread, captive cunt. She heard a high, keening sound and was dimly aware it must be her own voice. The tiny part of her brain that still functioned knew she was supposed to be silent, but she had lost all control of her body and her responses. On and on the powerful orgasm wracked her tortured, exhausted body, waves and waves of intensity as the cane continued to stroke her swollen, throbbing clit.

Finally Master John stepped back, leaving Alexis bathed in sweat and shuddering with post-orgasmic spasms, arms and legs spread wide and taut in her bonds. When she had finally stilled, completely spent, Master John unknotted and unwrapped the rope that bound her wrists and ankles.

Alexis was limp as a ragdoll as Master John lifted her into his arms and lay her down on a yoga mat on the floor near the table. Her head fell to the side, and after a while of drifting in a semi-conscious state, her eyes finally fluttered opened. Without a conscious decision to do so, she found herself looking to see if Master Paul was watching her. Would he approve?

He wasn't there.

Feeling suddenly bereft, Alexis turned her head back to face her trainer, who had crouched down beside her. She had to concentrate to focus on Master John, who was now speaking.

"I'm pleased, Alexis. You were holding back initially, but I think you're showing some potential. We'll keep working on associating pleasure and pain.

And I think, too, some focus on your ass is definitely in order to desensitize you in that area."

Alexis struggled to keep her feelings from her face, but realized she probably failed, as Master John's eyebrows rose, his lips tugging downward in a frown. "You have a problem with that?"

"No," Alexis said quickly, though it was a lie. "No, Sir."

"Good." Reaching into his pocket, Master John again produced her leash, which he clipped to her collar. "We have time for a shower before lunch," he said. "Right after your enema."

Chapter 7

"The concept here, Alexis," Master John said, "is to stop trying to anticipate or control the outcome. In just the little time we've spent together, you've made it clear you have issues with giving up control. If you ever want to get to that place where true submission is possible, you have to surrender, not just physically, not just mentally, but all of it. You have to give me everything you've got."

Alexis lay on a thick, soft towel that had been laid over the exam table in the slave quarters bathroom. She was glad at least that her face was to the wall during the procedure. She was lying on her side, her top leg drawn up toward her chest. Her hands were cuffed together in front of her, nestled between her breasts. The cuffs were clipped to a chain that attached to the O ring at the front of her collar.

Master John stood behind her. The enema bag had been prepared and hung on an IV pole. "First, we'll lubricate the area with Vaseline," he said. "I've found this works better than a water-based lubricant. Less irritation when the nozzle is removed." He put his hand on her hip, stroking her for a moment.

The hand was removed and she could hear the sounds of a latex glove snapping into place on his hand. "Lie still and relax."

Easy for you to say, Alexis couldn't help thinking, as she felt a finger, gooey with thick lubricant, rim her asshole and then slip inside. He moved slowly in a gentle swirling motion, and Alexis felt her body relaxing.

"Here's what's going to happen," Master John said, his finger still inside her ass. "I will insert the nozzle into your anus and slowly release the fluid. Your job is to relax and open yourself. Don't clench your muscles. Don't resist me in any way. Remember, this is about surrender. You aren't going to get to that place you seek until you truly surrender."

Finally he withdrew his finger. Alexis flinched a little when she felt the rubber nozzle between her ass cheeks.

"Take a deep breath and then let it out slowly," Master John said in a soothing voice. "That's it. In...and out..." As he spoke, Alexis felt the rubber head of the nozzle pushing past the ring of muscle and in spite of herself, she could feel her muscles clenching. As the nozzle pushed in deeper she squeezed her eyes shut.

Though Alexis was aware some people found enemas an erotic form of submission, for her the idea of an enema held zero appeal. Or more correctly, negative appeal. It wasn't just the thought of someone squirting a bunch of liquid directly into her intestines, but what came after. She would have to use the toilet, and she was almost certain Master John would stand there and watch her. Just the thought of this humiliation made her fingers curl into fists.

"Stop it." Master John's voice became stern. "I can feel your resistance. Open yourself to receive what I give you, not just physically, but mentally, too. You're untrained, I get that. So for now, just know I want this for you, and therefore you will accept it. Your ultimate goal as a submissive is not only to accept what your Master wants for you, but to embrace it precisely because he wants it."

Alexis took another deep breath and let it out slowly as she consciously tried to relax.

"Better."

Alexis felt a sudden, warm gush of liquid released inside of her.

"Oh!" she cried involuntarily.

"Breathe," Master John urged again. She felt another rush of warmth inside her, and then a sudden painful cramping in her intestines.

"It hurts. I think I have to go!" Alexis cried, her face flaming with embarrassment.

"Not yet," Master John said. "You've only taken about half the bag. You can take more. The cramping will ease. Deep breaths."

Alexis willed her body to accept what was

happening, praying she wouldn't have an accident right there on the table. It seemed to go on forever, but finally Master John said, "There. You took the whole bag. I'm going to remove the nozzle and replace it with a small butt plug." Alexis felt the nozzle being pulled slowly out and then the press of the plug into her still-relaxed anus.

Bending over her, Master John released her cuffs from her collar, but didn't remove the cuffs themselves. "Now," he informed her, "You're going to masturbate while I paddle your ass. Make sure not to push out that plug, or we'll have a nasty mess on our hands. Oh, and ask permission before you come."

Alexis had been sure he would let her up to relieve herself once she'd taken the enema. She lay there without moving, her mind trying to process what he'd just said. Make herself come? While being paddled? And lying on her side? Fuck!

"Get to it," Master John snapped, his words accompanied by a sudden sharp smack of a paddle against her right butt cheek.

Spurred into action, Alexis jerked her cuffed wrists downward and slipped the fingers of her right hand awkwardly between her legs. Despite the discomfort and embarrassment of enduring the enema, she was surprised to find she was soaking wet. As the paddle again made its hard contact with her ass, her clit stiffened beneath her fingers and a small cry issued from her lips, part pleasure, part pain.

When the paddle struck the rounded base of the

butt plug she grunted, her intestines protesting, her stomach gurgling. Forcing herself to ignore the cramping, she rubbed furiously at herself, the stinging smash of the paddle against her ass offset by the rising pleasure at her center.

"Oh, god," she moaned, her body shaking with her effort to push through the pain of the paddling as she rode her hand toward a climax. "Please, Sir. May I come?"

The paddle smashed against her even harder than before and she gave a gasping cry, tears filling her eyes. "Yes," he said, never letting up with the paddle while Alexis careened over the precipice of an unexpectedly powerful orgasm at her own hand.

The sting of the paddle was replaced by Master John's large, strong hands, his stroke surprisingly gentle and soothing against her burning flesh. "I am pleased," her trainer said as he stroked her ass and back. In spite of her exhaustion, Alexis's mouth lifted into a smile, his words sending a warm thrill of pleasure through her.

Master John allowed her to rest awhile, her cuffed hands still caught between her legs, until her breathing eventually slowed to something near to normal. "Sit up," he said eventually. "I'll help you off the table and take you to the toilet. You will crouch over the seat while I remove the plug. Then you may relieve yourself."

As he helped Alexis to a sitting position, her intestines again cramped painfully. All the pleasure of the orgasm and the warmth of his praise had evaporated. She desperately needed to use the toilet, but at the same time dreaded the prospect with Master John as witness.

Her hands still cuffed, Alexis was led by Master John to the row of toilets. At least they were the only two people in the communal bathroom, though that was still one too many.

Under Master John's unblinking gaze, Alexis straddled the toilet seat. He had a plastic bag in his hand. Reaching behind her, he pulled the plug and dropped it into the bag while Alexis lowered herself quickly to the seat.

Tears of embarrassment and shame pricked her eyelids as she expelled the enema liquid and her own waste in front of her trainer. At the same time, she couldn't deny the intense physical relief.

While she was relieving herself, Master John dropped the plastic bag into a utility sink near the shower stalls, stripped his gloves into the trashcan and then moved to the bank of sinks beneath the mirrors. After he'd washed his hands, he returned to Alexis, who was still sitting on the toilet.

Bending toward her, he unclipped the cuffs and removed them from her wrists. "Wipe yourself and take a shower," he instructed. "I'll see you in the dining room for lunch."

~*~

They were in a large, sumptuously furnished

room. The wood paneled walls were decorated with oil paintings of Impressionistic landscapes. A large crystal chandelier hung from the high, vaulted ceiling. It could have been any elegantly appointed drawing room, except for the St. Andrew's crosses flanking either side of a huge stone

fireplace. Several flogger and whip handles could be seen protruding from a tall brass umbrella stand. An end table beside it held an ice bucket, a small propane tank with a torch attached to the top of it and a black velvet pouch.

Alexis was kneeling on a cushion beside six other naked trainees, four women and two men. They were lined up in a row along one wall with a good view of the entire room. Alexis's ass was still tender from an extended caning session in the dungeon after lunch. She had been cuffed by her wrists to long chains that hung from the ceiling, her arms so high she'd had to stand on tiptoes for the duration of the caning. She had taken quite a beating, moving from the initial resistance to a kind of resigned, exhausted surrender, but without ever achieving the sense of release and peace that continued to remain just out of her grasp, even here at The Compound.

Several staff slaves were kneeling or sitting at the feet of the trainers who lounged on sofas and chairs scattered around the room. Alexis was keenly aware of the presence of Master Paul, who was on a sofa across the room. He was wearing a white shirt opened at the throat and jeans that hugged strong, muscular legs. Though she knew she shouldn't even be thinking this way, she was glad to note that, unlike many of the trainers scattered throughout the room, there was no one kneeling at his feet, no head resting proprietarily on his knee. Tiffany was kneeling in the row with Alexis, her back ramrod straight, a diamond piercing glinting at her belly button, a matching diamond stud nestled on one side of her pert little nose.

All eyes turned to the open double doors of the drawing room as Mistress Miriam entered the room. She was dressed in a flowing red gown, cut low to reveal a deep cleavage. Master John entered just behind her. He had changed from the black T-shirt and jeans he'd worn earlier in the day, and looked quite sexy in black leather pants and a vest over his muscular chest, which was covered in dark blond curls. Lastly came Wendy, wearing a see-through white shift that barely covered her slender, naked body. Her feet were bare, the gold heart-shaped padlock glinting at her throat.

Mistress Miriam, with Master John and Wendy next to her, stood in front of the fireplace and addressed the room. "We are gathered tonight to witness the branding ceremony of Master John and his slave girl, Wendy."

Turning to Wendy, Mistress Miriam said, "Slave Wendy, do you choose this permanent branding of your flesh of your own free will?"

Though Alexis thought she saw fear in Wendy's large gray eyes, her voice was firm as she answered, "Yes, Mistress."

"And with this brand," Mistress Miriam continued, "do you promise to love and serve Master John with your heart, body and soul until the time he releases you?"

"Yes, Mistress," Wendy replied, a radiant smile lighting her face as she gazed up at her Master.

Turning to Master John, Mistress Miriam said, "And you, John. With this brand do you claim permanent ownership of slave Wendy, promising to own and cherish her as long as you remain Master and slave?"

"I do," Master John intoned, as if taking a marriage vow. He took Wendy's small hand in his much larger one.

Mistress Miriam again addressed the room. "In order to help Wendy achieve the proper mindset for the intensity of the branding, her Master has chosen the meditation of a long, slow flogging. Through the whipping of the skin, Wendy will achieve an altered state, one which changes the very nature of pain and one's ability to bear it."

Mistress Miriam stepped to the side of the hearth while Master John selected a heavy black flogger from the umbrella stand. "Prepare yourself," he said to Wendy. Without hesitation the girl slipped the straps of her skimpy dress off her shoulders and let the shift puddle to the floor. Turning her smooth, naked body so she was in profile to the room, she lifted her arms over her head, clasping each wrist with the opposite hand. Wendy was thin but muscular and despite her grace and apparent ease, Alexis thought she detected some tension in the rigid way she held her body as she waited for her flogging to begin.

Alexis watched with hungry eyes as her trainer brushed the soft leather tresses over his slave girl's back. Wendy remained perfectly still as the first hard stroke landed between her shoulders. The sound of the leather making contact with skin was the only sound in the large room. Master John moved with skill behind the girl, the flogger whirling and striking her reddening skin from shoulder to thigh.

After about ten minutes of intense flogging, the change began to happen before Alexis's eyes. It was almost as if Wendy were sloughing off an old skin, her demeanor taking on a kind of ethereal glow. The muscles that had been clenched only a moment before eased and softened, though Wendy didn't move her position or lower her arms. Her head fell back, her lips parting, her eyes closing as if she were slipping into a deep, peaceful sleep, though she remained standing.

Alexis recognized what she was seeing, and ached inside with the knowledge she herself had yet to experience this kind of ecstatic transformation, and maybe never would.

Faith in your trainer. Faith in yourself.

Sam's words drifted into Alexis's mind as she watched Master John slow the flogging until it was once again a swishing, gentle stroke of soft leather. Was faith all that was required? And if so, where was hers? How did she find it, tap into it, harness it? Maybe someday it would be her up there, giving herself in public to her Master, her lover...

Mistress Miriam nodded toward a dark-skinned man sitting near the fireplace. The man stood and approached the stone hearth. "Master Clarence is our branding expert," Mistress Miriam said. "He will execute the branding, with Master John's assistance."

Mistress Miriam waved an imperious hand toward the men. "Gentlemen, you may proceed." She took the seat Clarence had vacated, and Marta scooted from a nearby spot to nestle against her knees. Mistress Miriam stroked Marta's head as if she were a favored pet.

Though Wendy still seemed to be in a trancelike state, she walked with a slow, graceful gait as Master John led her to the St. Andrew's cross on the right side of the hearth. As she leaned with her back against the cross, her expression was serene, almost vacant. With languid movements she raised her arms, resting them against the top half of the X.

Master John secured her wrists into the cuffs set there for the purpose, and then crouched to lock her ankles into the cuffs at the bottom. He wrapped a thick strap of leather around her waist to hold her still against the cross. Finally he took a cloth gag from his pocket. He pressed it into Wendy's open mouth and as she bit down, he tied it around the back of her head.

Master Clarence was holding the propane torch in his hand.

"Are you ready, slave girl?" Master John said, his voice low but audible as he addressed his lover.

Wendy nodded, her eyes fixed on his face.

Master John kissed the girl's forehead and then stepped back. He retrieved the velvet pouch and slipped what Alexis realized must be the branding tool from its confines. Taking a pair of insulated pliers Alexis hadn't noticed before from the table, he clamped the long, thin handle of the brand in its grip and handed the pliers to Master Clarence.

Master Clarence flicked on the propane torch, and a long, hot blue flame shot from the top of it. As he held the design end of the brand into the flame, Alexis glanced anxiously at Wendy. Some of her sensual languor seemed to have slipped away. Her eyes were wide and though she still appeared calm, her forehead and upper lip beaded with sweat.

When the brand was heated to a red-hot glow, Clarence lifted it from the flame and quickly set down the torch. "Now," he said, moving close to Wendy on the cross. Master John, who was standing on Wendy's other side, clamped his hand hard over Wendy's gagged mouth just as Master Clarence pressed the burning metal to her right inner thigh.

He held the brand in place for several long seconds. Even with the gag in place and Master John's hand firmly over her mouth, Wendy's small but agonized cry could be heard throughout the otherwise silent room. The smell of burning flesh reached Alexis's nostrils and for a second, she thought she was going to pass out.

While Master Clarence held ice over the burn, Master John removed the gag and used it to wipe the sweat and tears from his slave's face. Alexis was close enough to hear his murmured, "My brave girl. My good girl," as he unwound the thick leather strap from her waist and released the cuffs.

Though her face was very pale and her limbs trembled, Wendy wrapped her arms around Master John's neck. A spontaneous patter of applause and congratulations rippled through the room as Master John lifted his slave girl from the cross and turned with her in his arms. As he carried Wendy from the room, Alexis saw the angry red burn, a small sideways 8.

It was, she realized, the infinity sign, a symbol of ongoing, never ending love. Alexis touched her own thigh in the spot where Wendy had been branded and she sighed audibly, her heart aching with longing for that kind of connection with another person.

Several heads turned her way at her unplanned outburst, but it was Master Paul, his amber-gold eyes burning into hers, that made Alexis blush and look away.

The Compound

Chapter 8

I could be in my office right now, Alexis suddenly thought, reading the Wall Street Journal and sipping my first cup of coffee before checking my emails and attacking my inbox.

Instead she was naked and on her knees on the hard, cold bathroom tiles, scrubbing the floor with a huge sponge. As she spread the steaming water in soapy circles, she pondered her situation. Had she made a mistake in coming to The Compound? Should she just admit she wasn't of the same caliber as Wendy and Tiffany and probably never would be?

No! Don't be a quitter. This is where you're supposed to be. This is where you belong. Don't fuck up this chance to discover your potential. Rome wasn't built in a day.

The ferocity of her own silent response surprised her. But when she shut out the noise of insecurity and misplaced longings, she knew it was right. She deserved this amazing chance to connect with the submissive longings that had both propelled her and left her feeling a lack all her adult life.

As she worked, she stole a sidelong glance at Marta, who was at the grooming station with Linda, one of the trainees who had been kneeling near Alexis the night before at the branding ceremony. Linda was older than most of the trainees, probably in her fifties. Her heavy breasts sagged over a body marked by childbirth and a slowing metabolism, and yet she seemed completely relaxed in her imperfect nudity as Marta expertly groomed her. The two women chatted quietly while Marta worked, spreading hot wax, pressing squares of soft cloth and then ripping them away.

Alexis had been assigned to work with Marta that morning. Master John was taking the morning off to tend to Wendy, she had been informed by a different trainer, a woman called Mistress Elena, who had conducted Alexis's morning inspection in his stead.

"When you're done with the floor, you can clean the toilets," Marta called out to Alexis.

Can't wait, Alexis nearly said aloud. Instead she just nodded. Service is a form of submission. Do it with grace.

~*~

"Position 4," Paul said, pointing to his booted feet. Tiffany dropped at once to her knees and crawled with a sexy sway across the dungeon floor toward him. There was little work left to do with her. She was trained and ready, eager to meet the Master who was flying up from Texas to claim her. The man was due to arrive sometime today.

Contracts would be signed, money would exchange hands and Tiffany would leave The Compound with a man she'd never met.

Paul tried to imagine linking himself with a stranger, based solely on emails, videos and testimonials of her sexual submission, her physical appearance and her ability to endure erotic torture. James Bradley had paid Mistress Miriam a hefty sum to take Tiffany back to his home in Texas and Tiffany herself would also receive a sizable stipend, as it was referred to, once she had completed a six month contract with her new Master. At that time, they might negotiate her continued servitude, or she would be free to return to her former life, which Paul knew had been as a flight attendant for a major airline.

"Position 8b," Paul said, watching as the young woman pivoted so her pretty little bottom was facing him. She lowered her forehead until it touched the floor, her blond curls spilling over her shoulders. She reached back and spread her ass, revealing the tiny rosebud of her perfect asshole for his inspection.

She was twenty-four. James Bradley was forty-eight. They were strangers to each other, and yet she had committed six months of her life to him. Was this really what she wanted? To serve without love? To submit without passion?

Paul shook his head, silently berating himself for his romantic notions. The Compound was a professional training facility designed to teach potential subs and slaves how to submit with grace and honesty. Though much of the fixed costs of maintaining The Compound were covered by a hefty endowment from a wealthy patron, Paul knew Miriam relied on these slave placements and the fees they generated to keep the place running. Not everyone required love to serve or dominate. For many just the power of BDSM itself was enough to provide deep and lasting fulfillment.

Paul selected the largest butt plug on the tray. Mr. Bradley had been clear in his requirements about anal prep. Paul thought about their last phone conversation. Mr. Bradley's thick Texas accent almost seemed like a parody. "All my fillies got to wear their pony tails with pride, you understand me? Any girl that can't take it up the ass ain't got no place in Master B's stable."

Tiffany was fully aware she would be expected to be Bradley's pony slave, complete with her own harness, pony tail and mouth bit, and she didn't appear at all fazed at the prospect. It was a consensual arrangement, and everyone seemed perfectly happy with it. Who was Paul to pass judgment on anyone else for their choices?

Paul eased the huge, well-lubricated plug between Tiffany's pert ass cheeks, watching as the whole of it slipped into that tiny hole while the girl remained utterly still. He placed the specially-designed mouth bit between her teeth and buckled it behind her head. Finally he bound her arms behind her back with the leather sleeves that ran from shoulder to wrist.

"Prance," he ordered, and off Tiffany went,

walking around the dungeon in a slow, stiff-legged movement, lifting each foot high in imitation of a horse lifting its hooves.

She moved sedately and gracefully despite her getup, weaving between the training scenes already in progress at the various stations.

There's nothing left for me to teach her, Paul thought as he watched her. He couldn't deny the pride he felt at how she had blossomed under his tutelage. Though to be fair, she was a natural with a lot of prior experience before coming to The Compound. She had only needed minimal guidance and direction to achieve her full potential.

I wonder who I'll get next.

When he'd first arrived at The Compound eleven months ago, he'd been thrilled at the opportunity to hone his training skills, and to work with Miriam, whose reputation as a master trainer was international in scope. Disenchanted with the practice of law, he'd resigned from his law firm, prepared to live on his savings while he figured out what he wanted to do next.

The arrangement at The Compound was ideal — free room and board, plus a modest salary in exchange for six hours a day of BDSM training. Not to mention the perks, like use of the Olympic size pool and daily blowjobs without any relationship strings attached.

Relationships.

Though he'd been in a few of those complicated

entanglements over the past couple of years, so far no one had managed to penetrate the walls he'd built around his heart since his breakup with Jessica three years before. With the passage of time and the healing of his wounded ego, he realized even with Jessica it hadn't been love. Not the kind of all-consuming and committed love he knew was out there — somewhere.

The Compound had seemed the ideal place to fully exploit his dominant drive and sadistic urges without even having to think about the possibility of falling in love. Miriam's policy of trainers not getting romantically involved with their trainees made sense. It jived with his own belief that a certain emotional distance was necessary in this sort of environment. While he could appreciate a woman's beauty or submissive ability, he tended to view his trainees at a clinical remove, always aware that within a month or so they would return to their lives outside The Compound. There were exceptions of course, like Wendy and Marta, but even they were off limits during their initial training phase.

He looked around the dungeon as Tiffany moved with equestrian grace through the room. Where was Alexis this morning? The girl with the shiny dark hair and those lovely brown eyes?

Alexis.

How riveted she'd been while watching last night's ceremony. Even from across the room he had seen a flush of rosy color moving over her cheeks, the nipples on her luscious breasts perking and her lips parting as she watched John flog Wendy. He could almost feel the girl's longing, and in spite of himself, his cock had hardened as he watched her.

I want her.

There. He'd admitted it. He wanted to fuck her. He wanted to put her through her paces and see her grace firsthand. He wanted to be her trainer. No. Not her trainer. Her lover.

Whoa.

He thought back to her profile. She'd indicated she was single, and not involved in a committed relationship. When her training was over...? Would his interest be returned?

Tiffany had made her way around the perimeter of the dungeon and now returned to him, dropping into a graceful kneel before him, pressing her lips to the toe of his black boot. He stared at the top of her blond head, forcing himself to focus on her breathy murmur. "Thank you, Sir. Thank you, Master Paul."

~*~

Alexis's arms were spread wide on either side of her, tethered with soft rope knotted at her wrists, the other ends tied to sturdy branches between two trees. She was facing another new trainee named Rachelle, who was similarly bound.

There was a group of onlookers lying and sitting on a huge picnic blanket not far from the tree. The group included several trainers, a few trainees and a few of the staff slaves. They'd all come out for a picnic lunch near a stream at the back of the property, a good ten minute walk from the main house, hidden by a copse of trees. They had settled by an old barn, everyone chatting amiably as if it were perfectly natural for some of the group to be naked and collared, the rest fully clothed. Of course, Alexis realized, here on The Compound that was perfectly natural.

When Master John had told her they would be attending a picnic luncheon instead of eating in the dining room that afternoon, she had thought it would be fun and relaxing to eat outside by a rolling stream.

She hadn't expected to be the entertainment.

After Master John had fed her half a sandwich and some pieces of apple, he'd said casually, "Go stand between those two trees, Alexis."

Master Clarence had nodded to Rachelle, adding, "You too. Face Alexis and raise your arms. We'll see how well you two handle a little predicament bondage."

The two men stood beside them, and Master Clarence held up a bright orange dildo, each end shaped like a penis. It was easily two feet long. "This is my personal favorite," he informed both girls with an evil smile.

Master John produced a tube of lubricant. After coating both heads, he pressed one end of the gel-filled phallus into Alexis's pussy, while Master Clarence worked the other end between Rachelle's spread legs. The dildo was soft and yielding. It actually felt good, filling her up nicely, though the circumstances were too distracting for her to really enjoy it.

"That's the pleasure, now here's the pain." Master John reached into his pocket and produced two pairs of clover clamps. He handed a pair to Master Clarence, and they set

about clamping Rachelle's and Alexis's nipples, only instead of using a single pair on a single girl, Alexis's left nipple was tethered to Rachelle's right nipple, and vice versa.

"We're going to cane you both," Master John said. "You are expected to keep the dildo in place between you. If it falls out, no matter who is at fault, you will both be punished. And as I'm sure you know, when you tug on clover clamps, they only get tighter. So you both have strong motivation to remain as still as you can."

Rachelle and Alexis met each other's eyes and Rachelle offered Alexis a nervous smile. She was, Alexis saw, trembling slightly and the caning hadn't even begun. Rachelle was newer to all this than she was, Alexis realized. It was up to her to be a model sub. She would be an example for Rachelle. She would make Master John proud.

Hopefully.

Master John was behind Alexis, Master Clarence behind Rachelle, each holding a long, thin cane. They began lightly, warming the skin with a steady tapping, focusing mainly on the girls' bottoms. At the first hard stroke, both girls gasped. Alexis managed to stay still, but Rachelle's sudden jerk caused a painful tug to Alexis's nipples.

"Sorry," the girl mouthed, but at the next stroke she jerked again, tightening the clamps yet again.

Though she hadn't realized she was doing it, each stinging stroke of the cane caused Alexis to clench her muscles upon impact, and this included her vaginal muscles. Thus each fiery cut of the cane was matched by a thrust of pleasure rippling inside her cunt as she gripped the malleable cock buried inside her.

The cane strokes increased in both tempo and intensity. Alexis closed her eyes, willing herself to flow with the pain and focus on the pleasure. Rachelle was whimpering, her breathy cries getting louder. She began to jerk again, doing a kind of avoidance dance that pulled the chains between the clover clamps taut again and again, tugging hard at Alexis's already tortured nipples.

To make matters worse, a sudden sideways move by Rachelle nearly caused the dildo to be pulled from Alexis's pussy. Alexis tried to get the girl's attention, but Rachelle had her eyes closed. If she didn't get control of herself, the dildo was going to fall out.

Determined not to let this happen, Alexis tried to mirror Rachelle's moves, stepping forward as Rachelle stepped back, arching her hips or twisting in an effort to keep the dildo in place between them. She was restricted somewhat by the ropes at her wrists, but there was enough play to allow the tortured dance between them to continue.

At one point the dildo very nearly slipped out, saved only by Alexis lunging forward as Rachelle jerked back. This isn't my fault! Alexis wanted to scream. She was handling the caning and enduring the tight grip of the clamps. She was doing her best to remember everything Master John had taught her. She was flowing with the pain. She was staying quiet and still, but Rachelle was yelping and dancing on her toes. She was going to ruin everything. The girl had no discipline, and Alexis was going to pay the price.

Though Master John continued to cane Alexis, she saw Master Clarence lower his cane as he leaned down and whispered something in Rachelle's ear. As he spoke, he stroked her cheek with two fingers. Whatever he said must have worked, because to Alexis's relief, the girl stopped her panicked flailing. She lowered herself from her toes and the tension eased out of her shoulders.

Master Clarence again resumed the caning. The girl whimpered but she remained still, save for the swivel of her hips. It wasn't long before she began to shudder, her pelvis gyrating in time to the strokes of the cane and Alexis realized finally what was happening. Rachelle was jerking herself off on the dildo! She was going to orgasm, while Alexis was forced to move in tandem to keep the other end of the phallus in place and minimize the painful tug at her nipples.

"Please, Master Clarence, may I come?" the girl cried. "You may," he replied in his deep bass.

No fair, Alexis thought. That wasn't part of the deal.

Master Clarence had lowered his cane to let the girl climax, but Master John continued to cane Alexis's stinging, tender ass and thighs. Finally the girl's pelvic gyrations eased, and mercifully, Master John, too, lowered his cane.

Alexis was startled by the laughter and applause coming from the picnic blanket. She had almost forgotten they had an audience. When she turned, he was there! Though he definitely hadn't been part of the lunch group, Master Paul was lying on his side on the picnic blanket, leaning up on his elbow. Tiffany was nowhere in sight.

Alexis felt a slow burn move over her skin and tingle in her cunt as they locked eyes. A sensual smile moved over his features, lifting the corners of his mouth and radiating at the corners of his eyes.

Alexis forced herself to look away—to focus on her trainer. Master John released the clover clamps, and Alexis couldn't stop her gasping yelp as a jolt of agonizing pain shot through her nipples.

Master John led Alexis back to the blanket, and as she settled herself gingerly to minimize her sore bottom's contact with the blanket, he poured a glass of cold lemonade from a thermos and handed it to her. As she drank, Alexis was hyper-aware of Master Paul just a few feet away, but she managed to keep her eyes on her trainer.

"You did well, Alexis," Master John said, bestowing on her one of his rare smiles. "The circumstance was difficult, yet you held your ground. I'm pleased."

His praise was like a soothing balm. Alexis smiled gratefully. "Thank you, Sir."

"Thank me properly," he replied, pointing to his boot.

Embarrassed she'd forgotten this bit of protocol, Alexis knelt quickly forward, pressing her lips to the dusty toe of his leather boot. "Thank you, Sir," she said again.

"You may rise," he said imperiously after a moment. As Alexis stood, she saw the others were also getting to their feet. Master Clarence and Rachelle were still by the tree, talking softly.

Master John glanced at his watch and turned to Master Paul. "Are you free right now?"

Master Paul, who had also stood, nodded. "Yeah. Tiffany's new Master arrived at lunch. He asked if he could keep her for the afternoon, so I've got nothing but time. What can I do for you?"

"I want to check on Wendy," Master John replied. "She's resting in the cottage today. Could you take Alexis back to the dungeons? If you were interested, I could use some help with her training exercise this afternoon."

Master Paul glanced at Alexis, his expression difficult to read. Turning back to Master John, he replied, "Sure. It would be my pleasure."

Chapter 9

When James Bradley arrived earlier than planned during lunch and asked for the afternoon alone with Tiffany, Paul thought he'd spend time in his room catching up on emails and doing some research for his upcoming vacation.

Instead, aware that some of the staff were having a picnic by the old barn, and aware that John, and more specifically Alexis, would be among them, he decided to take a walk around the grounds. And he just happened to find himself heading toward the picnic spot.

He had come upon a delicious predicament bondage scene, drinking in the sight of two lovely women tied between two trees, a double-headed dildo between them, clamp chains swaying as they danced and squirmed at each swishing strike of the cane. When he'd realized one of them was Alexis, his cock sprang to attention, and he had to keep his distance for a while until he got control of himself.

It was at that moment he couldn't lie to himself anymore. He was smitten with a trainee! This was something he'd managed to avoid so far during his tenure at The Compound. Sure, he'd developed an intense connection during the training period with each submissive—that kind of connection was inevitable when you were involved in such an intimate process.

And yes, some of the women he'd trained were seriously hot. But even when he'd been sexually attracted to his charges, he'd managed to keep his feelings pretty well in check. The connection, in the end, was really more of a physical reaction than an emotional one—a welding of his hardwiring as a Dom to their hardwiring as a sub. And, as jaded as it must sound to someone on the outside, submissive naked slave girls were a dime a dozen at The Compound. You got used to them, if such a thing was possible.

So what was it about Alexis that got his cock hard every time he saw her? It wasn't just her physical beauty. There was more to it.

Some of the sentences in her essay had lodged themselves into his memory, fitting themselves like a missing puzzle piece into a groove in his soul. *I have spent a lifetime building a wall around my true submissive nature, brick, by brick, by brick. And now, when I have finally found the courage to face my need and embrace my longing, I find I don't have the tools.*

He felt a kindred affinity with her words, and by extension, with her. For hadn't he done the same thing, in a way? Not that he'd denied his dominant impulses, but he'd never truly given of himself, not in the way he envisioned in the kind of D/s relationship he longed for.

He knew how to give a sub the tools to submit with grace and honesty. He knew how to use a whip and a cane, how to spark submissive desire and how to harness and control it. But when it came to himself, to a true exchange of power rather than just his taking it from another, he'd always held himself back. Even with Jessica, who he'd thought for a while was "the one", he'd never fully given himself to her, and on some level they both had known this. He'd never given his heart.

It was, he realized, a matter of trust. How ironic that the very thing he demanded of his trainees was something he himself was unable to give. Could it be he'd just never found the right person?

He knew he was infatuated with Alexis, but also knew infatuation was a far cry from love. He would have to get to know her better to see if there was even a potential for that kind of connection. And for that, he would have to wait. The trainees were off limits, and with good reason. He understood and respected Miriam's strict policy of not fraternizing with the trainees during their training period. But once the training was over...

Down boy, he told himself. Alexis had only been at The Compound for a short time. And she was signed up for a whole month. That meant he needed to keep his professional distance from her until then. At least he knew from her profile that she wasn't involved in a relationship at present. That gave him a shot. He would have to be patient and bide his time. And hope his interest in her was returned.

The other trainers were leading their trainees by their leashes across the broad expanse of meadow. Alexis looked at him with a questioning glance as he waited for the others to go on ahead. Miriam had instructed the trainers that the trainees should be led by their leashes whenever they were together outside, though when the trainees were alone, they were free to roam unleashed. Paul was tempted to dispense with the leash and just walk side by side, but he realized that wouldn't be fair to Alexis. The object of Miriam's rigorous training program included total immersion into the submissive slave mindset. To suddenly treat Alexis as an equal would be a disservice to her.

And so he said, "Present the leash." Alexis dropped at once to the grass and placed the end of the leash on her upturned palms. She lifted her arms, offering the leash to him, her eyes properly downcast. The trainer in him came to the fore and he said, "Try that again. Imagine you're moving in water. It's a slow, controlled motion. You don't want to just flop to the ground like that."

He was amused to see color move over her cheeks as she stood. This time she lowered herself with more grace, though there was still room for improvement. No doubt John would work with her on positions training until she executed them as flawlessly as Wendy.

This time Paul accepted the offered leash and gave it a gentle tug, signaling that she should rise. Again, her movements could use some work, but he let it go. As they began to walk back toward the buildings,

Paul said, "Master John shared your profile with me. I found your essay quite moving."

"Oh." Again that sweet rosy blush bloomed on her cheeks.

Paul continued, "I remember you said something about building a brick wall around your true submissive nature. Is Master John managing to knock down some of the bricks yet? Is this immersion training what you expected?"

She would have been instructed to obey every trainer as if he were her Master. This meant she would know not to speak unless spoken to, but by the same token, she was to answer every question put to her with directness and honesty.

"I—I don't know. I mean, it's very intense. Master John is very, um..." she paused.

"Exacting?" Paul supplied, grinning.

"Yeah. I mean, yes, Sir." She smiled shyly, and something snapped inside Paul's heart, like a tiny bone breaking.

Ignoring the ache, he said, "He's a good trainer. He gets good results. I'm looking forward to working with the two of you this afternoon." Talk about an understatement, he thought, glad Alexis was behind him, and couldn't see his grin, or the anticipatory bulge in his jeans.

~*~

"Get on your knees and place your hands flat on the table in front of you, wrists touching." They were in the training dungeon for the extended afternoon session. "Spread your legs." Master John tapped Alexis's thigh. "Wider."

Master Paul had led Alexis back to the slave quarters after the picnic. On the walk back she had wished she wasn't on a leash several paces behind him. She would have liked to walk next to him. To take his hand and look into his eyes. Still, this way she did get a very nice view of his broad back and long, muscular legs. His jeans were just tight enough to show the curve of his sexy ass as he walked.

It would be my pleasure.

Did he mean it would be his pleasure to help out a friend? Or would it be his pleasure to subject her to some new erotic torture? Did he feel the same zing of recognition and desire she did when their eyes interlocked?

Silently she admonished herself at this ridiculous line of thinking. They weren't in high school, for god's sake. They were professionals, doing a job. Admittedly, a very sexy and exciting job, but she was just another trainee in a long line of them. She had been assigned to Master John, not Master Paul. He was there to help in the training, but she mustn't assign anything more to it than that.

The men had her climb up a set of portable stairs and position herself on a high, padded square table on her hands and knees, ass high in the air, legs spread wide. Though she'd been naked ever since she'd arrived at The Compound, with Master Paul

standing just behind her, she was especially aware of the picture she must present, with her waxed pussy and exposed asshole on full view.

"This afternoon we're going to subject you to full sensory deprivation. I want all distractions removed. As you won't be in a position to speak, if you find yourself in acute distress, you will open and close your hands." He turned toward the wall and called, "Sam. We need you." When Sam approached, Master John said, "You will assist us with this exercise as a spotter. If Alexis is in acute distress, she will open and close her hands. If we don't seem to notice, it's your job to alert us."

"Yes, Sir," Sam said. He crouched in front of Alexis and offered an encouraging smile.

Master John continued, "Alexis, you will not orgasm, no matter how stimulated you might find yourself. Is that clearly understood?"

"Yes, Master John." Alexis's stomach was clenched in nervous anticipation, and she couldn't stop the shudder of apprehension that moved through her body. While she was excited that Master Paul was there, he made her doubly nervous. Despite trying to talk herself out of it, she cared, really cared, what he thought of her.

A vibrator was eased inside her and flicked on, its thrum vibrating through her pussy and tickling her clit from the inside out. Reflexively she stiffened when she felt the lubricated tip of a butt plug probing her asshole, but willed herself to relax as it was pressed inside. To her surprise, the plug was also a vibrator, which hummed in tandem with the phallus in her cunt, the combined vibrations sending a shivery sensation through her loins.

Master Paul wrapped rope around her wrists, knotting it and pulling the long end back and up between her legs. He arranged it snugly between her pussy lips, pressing the vibrating plug and dildo even deeper into her holes. She could feel a little bump in the rope just where it lay over her clit, and realized it must be knotted at that strategic location, no doubt on purpose.

Master Paul leaned in close as he worked. He smelled good, like warm bread and pine forests. He was so close, if she turned her head she could brush his skin with her lips. She kept her head down.

Someone grabbed her hair, twisting it into a ponytail. She could feel the rope being tied into her hair, which forced her to lift her head to avoid having her hair pulled. Master Paul tied a blindfold over her eyes, while Master John pushed a ball gag into her mouth. Finally, she felt something soft pressed first into one ear and then the other.

Earplugs, she realized, as the world went silent.

They began with a flogger, focusing on her ass and back, the lovely soft leather stroking her body in a stinging caress. Each time she jerked in response, the ropes tightened against her cunt, the little knot at her clit moving like a raspy, rough tongue. Unable to see, speak or hear made the experience especially intense. She was unable to anticipate, and found this put her more directly into the moment than she'd ever been.

Without the distraction of sight or sound she was especially sensitive to the vibrations radiating from inside her body, and to the increasingly hard strokes of the flogger.

A sudden, sharp line of fire moved over her ass, making Alexis jerk in her bonds. She bit down hard on the rubber ball, grunting against it in her shock and pain. A second fiery kiss hissed along her flesh, just below the first and again she jerked, causing the rope to tighten against her spread pussy and tug hard against her tethered hair. Her heart was beating loud in her plugged ears and she felt herself sway, suddenly dizzy.

The flogging continued unabated, covering her back and shoulders, while what she realized must be a single tail snapped painfully against her ass and the backs of her thighs. If things got too intense to bear, she would flex her fingers, as Master John had said she could. But that would be giving up. She willed herself to stay in position, to make both Master John and Master Paul proud of her endurance and obedience.

A little longer, she urged herself. Just a little longer. You can do it. Master John said he wouldn't give you more than you could take. Trust him. Trust yourself. Let go.

On and on the dual whipping continued, while the vibrators thrummed inside her, and the rope jerked against her sex. She was whimpering steadily against the ball gag, drool leaking from the corners of her mouth. Sweat had broken out under her arms and on her forehead and she could feel the tremble beginning in her arms and legs.

Her skin began to numb beneath the onslaught of the flogger and the tail, and her focus shifted to her cunt. Her clit was throbbing, stroked by the knotted rope from without, and the vibrating phalluses filling her from within. She realized she was edging toward an orgasm, and further realized there wasn't a thing she could do about it.

You will not orgasm, Master John had informed her, as if not doing so was simply an act of will. Maybe it was. Maybe, if she tried, she could stave off the climax that seemed to be rising inside of her as inexorably as a wave crashing toward the shore.

She shifted her focus back to the whipping, to each cutting flick of the single tail, and each sensual thudding caress of the flogger. She thought about the men who were doing this to her — Master John, with his blond, all-American good looks and those round, unblinking eyes. He was probably the one with the single tail, she decided, casually welting her ass and thighs with each vicious flick of his wrist. Master Paul would be holding the flogger, his lovely golden-brown eyes moving over her bound, spread body as he whipped the leather tresses in a stinging symphony of sensation over her skin. Her clit throbbed at the image of Master Paul, his auburn hair glinting in the dungeon light as he danced around her.

Fuck. She was going to come.

Gritting her teeth, Alexis forced all images from her mind, trying to visualize a white, empty expanse of pure nothing. She would not come. She would not give in to her trembling body or her throbbing clit. Focus on the pain. Focus on your breathing. Focus on the pounding of your heart and the cut of the whip against your skin.

Maybe this was it. Maybe she would finally achieve that out of body experience she had heard and read so much about. Maybe today, on this padded table, roped and stuffed, deaf, dumb and blind, she would finally move to that exalted plane of existence where there was no difference between pleasure and pain, where her spirit soared beyond the confines of her body.

She was jerked from this line of thought by the feeling of hands, warm, strong hands moving over her tender and welted ass and thighs. Were they Master Paul's or Master John's? Who was touching her with such a soothing, sensual stroke? Despite herself, her mind veered to an image of Master Paul, his eyes burning into hers, his lips parting as he leaned toward her, his hands roaming her body as he lifted himself over her and bent down to kiss her lips. She was no longer on her knees, bound in rope in a training dungeon. She was lying on a bed on soft white sheets. Paul was naked, lifting his strong, sexy body over her as he nudged between her legs with his hard, perfect cock.

When he entered her in her imagination, she exploded in one of the most powerful orgasms of her life. As she shuddered and writhed in helpless release, she was dimly aware that the flogger was no longer sweeping her back. The hands that had caressed her skin had been removed. Only the battery-powered phalluses continued to work their relentless magic inside of her.

Finally the spasms subsided and her brain flicked back on. There was no way the two guys didn't know what had just happened. Two words flew into her brain.

Oh shit.

Chapter 10

"Not much self-control, eh?"

Those were the first words Alexis heard, once the earplugs were removed, Master Paul the one to utter them. Though he was standing behind her, Alexis imagined she could hear a smile in his voice.

"Very little," Master John replied, not a trace of humor in his tone. "I think a time out in the punishment closet is in order."

They untied her and lifted her from the bondage table. Alexis was too humiliated to do or say anything. How did the other subs control their bodies, and most especially their orgasms, with such apparent ease? Why couldn't she do that?

The punishment closet. Just the words filled her with jittery apprehension. Though not exactly claustrophobic, Alexis was not fond of confined spaces. She thought of begging for another chance, of dropping to her knees, wrapping her arms around Master John's legs and promising to do better if only he wouldn't punish her.

She didn't though, aware it would only make things worse. Courage, she told herself. She thought about her first meeting with Master John, and how he'd promised that, while he would push her boundaries, he wouldn't give her more than she could handle. She clung to the memory of this promise now, praying she would be able to handle whatever was to come.

Master Paul stepped into her line of vision, an expression of bemused sympathy on his face. Without speaking to her, Master John clipped a leash to Alexis's collar and gave it a yank, leading her, stumbling, from the dungeon.

He took her to a room just down the hall. Opening the door, he said, "You will spend the next hour in here. You need a time-out to ponder your lack of obedience and self- control." A single naked bulb glowed from a ceiling fixture. One wall of the tiny, windowless room was lined with large hooks from which hung coils of rope of different thicknesses, as well as chains and leather cuffs. A video camera was mounted in a corner, the lens pointed toward a yoga mat that covered most of the floor space.

Master John unclipped the leash and folded it into his pocket. "Lie on the mat face down. Then pull your knees up under your stomach and place your arms on the mat alongside your legs, each wrist touching an ankle, ass toward the door."

Alexis lay down meekly and tucked her legs underneath her body as ordered. Master John grabbed a coil of rope and began binding her right arm to her right leg from elbow

to wrist, and then doing the same on her left side, tying her down in a compressed bundle.

"You will be monitored via the camera to make sure you aren't in distress. You will not join us in the dining room this evening. A staff slave will come get you when your time out is over, and you can eat in the kitchen with the kitchen staff. In the meantime, I want you to ponder the nature of obedience and self-control. Think about why you're in the punishment closet, and what you can do to stay out of here in the future."

She heard the door close and realized she was alone. She had to bite her lip to keep from calling out, from begging him to let her out, not to leave her alone. After a minute or so, Alexis let out a little mewling whimper. She found she had clenched her hands into fists.

"Don't panic," she whispered aloud. She forced her fingers to uncurl. Take deep, slow breaths. She drew air deep into her lungs and let it out in a long, shuddery breath. After several of these breaths, she did actually begin to calm herself a little. She was safe, she reminded herself. She was being watched, and no one would let her come to any real harm.

She lifted her head, trying to shake the hair from her face and then resettled her cheek against the mat. She closed her eyes, continuing to focus on her breathing. She flexed her fingers, slowly opening and closing them. When she was calm enough to think, she tried to do as Master John had said, and ponder what had brought her to the punishment closet.

Though she was tempted to blame Master John and Master Paul for making her orgasm, she knew that wasn't a useful line of thinking. Why was control of her orgasm so hard for her? Why couldn't she seem to do what appeared to come so effortlessly for others?

She thought about dinner, about the empty cushion beside Master John's chair that night, and again her eyes pricked with tears of shame and not a little self pity. Would everyone know the reason for her absence? Master Paul would know. He had witnessed her lack of control.

It was so unfair. How was she expected to resist his touch, his scent, her own longing? This was Master Paul's fault.

Stop. Not useful, she reminded herself.

It occurred to her it was a good thing Master Paul wasn't her trainer. She was too sexually attracted to him to focus on the lessons of self control, discipline and obedience she knew were essential if she was to learn to be a proper submissive. He was definitely too much of a distraction. She was lucky, she told herself, to have been assigned to Master John. She wasn't in the least attracted to him, and anyway, he was in love with Wendy.

She thought about trying to roll over onto her side, but decided she'd better stay put in the position Master John decreed for her. At least the panic at being bound and left in this small space had subsided to a manageable degree.

The rope wasn't over-tight, and she was reasonably comfortable, though she would have liked to empty her bladder, and her nose was itching. She twisted her head, trying to use the mat to scratch her nose, but it didn't work too well. Her right foot began to cramp. Relax, she told herself. Carefully she arched the cramping foot, willing her muscles to ease.

Finally, with a sigh, she laid her cheek again against the mat and closed her eyes. She was exhausted in both body and mind by the ordeals of the day, and her ass and back felt flayed and tender. She would have loved to climb into a hot bath and soak for an hour, and then slip into her bed and sleep...

Alexis awoke to the sound of the door opening, for a moment confused to find she couldn't move at all. Her hands and feet had fallen asleep, she realized, and her cheek was wet from the drool that had puddled from her open mouth against the mat.

She heard someone moving behind her and then saw bare feet and slender legs appear in her line of vision, the skin a smooth bronzed cinnamon. Twisting her head, she saw it was Marta.

Kneeling beside her, Marta unwound the ropes from Alexis's cramped limbs and helped her to roll to a sitting position. Alexis wiped her mouth and shook back her hair. "Not much room in here," Marta observed. "Stand up and do some stretching exercises to get the blood flowing again."

Alexis took Marta's offered hand, allowing the young woman to pull her upright. Her feet and hands were tingling like mad as they came awake. She lifted her arms high over her head and then brought them behind her back in a stretch, while stepping from one foot to the other to stamp away the tingle.

Marta led Alexis down the back stairs that came out by the kitchen. After a quick stop in the powder room, they entered the large kitchen and were assailed by the heavenly scent of roasted meat and baked apples. Two male staff slaves, their bodies covered with white bibbed aprons, were moving about the kitchen, putting things away and loading a large dishwasher.

One of the men pointed to a high butcher block table. "Sit. I'll bring your plates." He turned toward a huge oven and pulled open its door. Taking two plates from inside, he set them on the table in front of the girls while the other guy placed a napkin at each plate, topping them with a knife and fork. He placed glass goblets beside each plate and filled them with cold water.

Alexis's stomach rumbled as she looked down at a plate loaded with pork tenderloin, sliced baked apples and steamed broccoli with a lemony sauce spooned over it. She looked questioningly at Marta. "Do we serve ourselves?" Since she'd been at The Compound, she'd gotten used to kneeling at her trainer's feet, waiting patiently to be fed from his fork or spoon.

"Yes. I'm sorry." Marta offered a sad smile.

Alexis understood then that this meal was in fact another part of her punishment. And by default, Marta had been dragged into it, and deprived of her chance to be fed at the hand of her Mistress. "I'm the one who's sorry," Alexis said.

Marta lifted her delicately arched eyebrows. "For?"

"I took you away from Mistress Miriam. You should have been with her, kneeling on your cushion, accepting her gift."

Marta shook her head. "No, Alexis. This is exactly where I'm supposed to be right now."

"Huh? I don't get it. Why should you have to suffer because I screwed up?"

"I'm not suffering." She placed a hand gently over Alexis's hand. "It pleases my Mistress that I'm here now with you. And so this is exactly where I'm supposed to be. More than that, it's where I want to be, for you, for her, and for myself."

Tears sprang to Alexis's eyes at this simple, sweet declaration. Blinking them away, she picked up her knife and fork and tucked into the delicious food. They ate quietly, each apparently absorbed with her own thoughts. Once the worst of Alexis's hunger had been satisfied, she turned again to Marta. "Can I ask you a question?"

Marta put down her knife and fork and wiped her mouth daintily with her napkin. "Sure."

"There's something I just don't get. Master John keeps talking to me about control. First he says I have to give over my control to him. Then he says I have to exercise self control. I'm supposed to let go and get out of my own way, but at the same time I'm supposed to keep hold of myself so I don't, like, you know, come without permission, for example." She shrugged, a little embarrassed. "I don't get it. I mean, how do I do both? Give up control and maintain control?"

Marta tilted her head a little, studying Alexis, an enigmatic smile moving over her lips. "Well, I can only speak for myself, but I think you need to frame it differently. I think maybe it's the language that's tripping you up." She wrapped her arms around her torso as she spoke, which caused her small, round breasts to lift and press together, drawing Alexis's eye to the small gold hoops that pierced each plump, dark nipple. She wanted to ask if the piercing had hurt, but forced herself to pay attention to what Marta was saying, aware she could learn something from this graceful and highly trained slave.

"It's not about giving up control per se," Marta continued. "It's more about trust — about trusting your Mistress or Master to guide you. It's about letting them direct your experience. It's still your experience. I mean, the goal isn't to become some kind of robot or Stepford Wife who does whatever is commanded without any thought or will of your own. It's more like a process of relinquishing control with a conscious grace — of trusting that they know what you want and need, sometimes even better than you do."

She smiled suddenly, her face taking on a radiant glow. "Even little things, like being fed by your Mistress—that's just another step in the journey of submission. I mean, think about it! You're trusting another person to provide you sustenance. It doesn't just feed your body, it feeds your soul."

"Oh," Alexis said softly, for now she understood Marta's earlier sad smile. The privilege wasn't in being allowed to sit at the table using one's own knife and fork—the real privilege was in being welcomed at your Master's feet, of receiving food and drink at his loving hand. For the first time she began to really understand the concept of submission that went beyond the sexual. A submission that offered an abiding comfort and even love.

~*~

The next morning after breakfast found Alexis back in the dungeon with Master John. She was perched on the edge of a stool that rested against a whipping post, her arms bound over her head to the post. Her legs were spread wide, her feet flat on the floor. Sam was crouched between her knees, his hands resting on her thighs.

"Know what this is?" Master John held up a black plastic wand tipped with a metal point not unlike a dentist's drill.

"Yes, Sir," Alexis replied, her eyes widening and her mouth going suddenly dry. "Have you ever experienced the shock of an electric prod firsthand?"

"No, Sir," she whispered faintly.

"It's an excellent operant conditioning tool. When you misbehave, you receive a shock, like so." He touched the sharp metal point to Alexis's arm, delivering a painful jolt of electricity. She squealed in pain and surprise.

"This morning," he said as if nothing had just happened, "we will work on control. If you hope to be a successful submissive, it's essential you learn to control yourself. Sam's going to lick your cunt until I tell him to stop. You are not to come until I give you express permission. Each time you feel yourself getting there, ask me for permission. If I say no, you will not come. Are we crystal clear on this?"

Alexis couldn't take her eyes off the ominous prod he was waving casually to punctuate his words. "Yes, Sir," she whispered.

"Good. Sam, begin."

Gripping Alexis's thighs, Sam pushed them wider and leaned forward. He licked along Alexis's outer labia and swirled his tongue in a tantalizing circle around her clit. In spite of her apprehension regarding the prod, his teasing touch felt wonderful, and Alexis almost relaxed against the whipping post as she gave in to the wet, hot pleasure of his tongue against her sex. The eroticism was heightened by her position, with arms extended and bound over her head, and legs spread wide, and it wasn't long before she felt the warm, buttery rise of a climax.

She looked to Master John, who was watching her carefully, the prod still in his right hand. Trying not to focus on the prod or anticipate its shocking touch, she managed to gasp, "Please, Sir, may I come?"

"No."

Before she realized what he was doing, Master John leaned toward her with the prod, touching the sharp metal tip to her left nipple.

Alexis screamed, the climax rapidly receding. "Go on, Sam. Don't stop what you're doing." "Yes, Sir," Sam replied.

Alexis again felt the warm, lapping stroke of Sam's tongue against her pulsing clit. Her nipple still throbbed from the painful electric shock, but after a minute the pleasure continued to mount, while the pain receded. Again it wasn't long before she felt the shuddering swell of an impending orgasm. Again she gasped, "Please, Master John. May I come?"

"No."

He zapped her other nipple, and again the pleasure was eclipsed by the sharp prick of the electric shock.

Again and again the process was repeated, until Alexis was trembling uncontrollably, her skin damp with sweat, her ragged breathing making her chest heave. "I can't," she panted, nearly crying. "No more, please!"

"You can. You will." Zap. Scream. Pant. Tongue.

Soothing, lovely, relentless tongue easing away the pain on her nipples, the underside of her breasts, her hip, her thigh.

"Oh god!" she cried, as her tender, swollen clit throbbed beneath Sam's touch. "Please, Sir, pleasepleasepleaseplease may I come!"

"Yes."

Though she heard him, her body took a second longer to react, tensing in anticipation of the prod. But then it caught up, and she felt herself careen headlong into an orgasm, with Sam kissing, licking and suckling for all he was worth. Alexis bucked, her body lifting entirely from the stool, all her weight on her wrists as she writhed in a pleasure that bordered on pain, it was so intense.

"No, yes, oh god, stop, don't stop, help me, oooooh..."

Sam didn't stop until Master John said quietly, "That's enough, Sam."

At once he leaned back on his haunches. Alexis, her heart pounding, sagged hard against her wrist cuffs, her pussy throbbing, her body wracked in a series of aftershock orgasmic spasms.

As Sam moved away, Master John moved close and unclipped Alexis's cuffs. He caught her in his arms as she fell forward, steadying her on the stool and then lifting her into his arms. He carried her toward a sofa set against one of the dungeon walls and lowered her gently to the cushions.

He sat beside her, stroking her hair from her face. "I am pleased. You are showing progress." He offered a rare smile, adding, "There's hope for you yet."

Chapter 11

Paul lifted the brandy snifter to his lips and took a long sip. It felt good as the heat of it spread through his chest. Since Tiffany's training was done and he hadn't yet been given a new assignment, he just listened as the other trainers reviewed their current assignments and discussed the progress of their trainees.

When John began to talk, Paul perked up. "She is making progress," John was saying, "but there remains a core resistance. It's like she can get so far and then, wham, we come up against a wall."

"The brick wall she referenced in her essay," Miriam offered with a smile. "Marta has befriended her. I do believe Alexis is sincere, but it's possible she just doesn't have whatever that submissive gene is that allows one to truly let go."

"She does. I think she does," Paul found himself interjecting more forcefully than he'd intended. He thought about the scenes he'd witnessed and been a part of with the lovely young woman. In a calmer tone, he elaborated, "I agree with John about her resistance, but she's still early on in her training. Don't forget, she comes more from a scene perspective. You know, the artificial construct of an impersonal BDSM scene at a club. She's still getting used to the all-encompassing experience of The Compound. She needs to achieve a certain comfort level so she can truly let go."

Miriam regarded him with a discerning glance, her mouth quirking in a half smile. "You certainly seem well-informed about John's trainee, Paul."

Paul felt his face heating. "Oh, well," he said lamely. "John shared her profile with me. And he invited me to participate in an exercise the other day." The compelling image of Alexis naked on the bondage table, the rope drawn taut against her cunt, the shudder and tremble of her body as they whipped her to a frenzy while the vibrators inside her did their work, leaped in blazing detail into his mind. He had felt her tension, her lust, her aching desire to submit, to obey, to endure what they gave her. It had been almost as if he'd had a direct conduit into her heart and mind. They'd been connected in a way that had startled him. He'd said nothing about this to anyone, certainly not to John, instead just storing it away for contemplation when he was alone in his room that night.

He was, he knew, falling for this girl. Falling hard.

Paul realized his cock had hardened at the memory of that scene. He shifted in his chair and crossed his legs. John and the other trainers were regarding him now with

quizzical stares. Embarrassed, Paul lifted his

glass and took another healthy swig of the brandy.

But Miriam wasn't ready to let him off the hook. "Tell us more, Paul. Are you suggesting you have a special connection with this trainee? Something Master John hasn't been able to tap into on his own?"

"No, I didn't mean—"

"There might be something to that," John interrupted in his calm, careful way. "She seems to respond with more authenticity when Paul is around, whether just as an observer or a participant. It could be he might have more success with her as her trainer."

Miriam seemed to ponder this a moment. Then she slowly shook her head. "I don't think that's necessary, unless you're unhappy with her, John?"

"No. I enjoy working with her. It's a challenge to push past all the shields. And what she lacks in experience, she does make up for in enthusiasm."

"Perhaps, especially now while he has no formal assignment, Paul could be an assistant." She turned to Paul. "What do you think?"

"Oh, I, um, I'm not sure..." He trailed off, annoyed with himself for being so inarticulate.

Miriam leaned over and patted his arm, as if she were in on the turmoil of his thoughts. "Paul," she said gently. "This isn't about you. It's about what's best for Alexis. I'm sure that whatever feelings you might have for this girl, you're professional enough to keep them at bay, for her sake. Am I right?"

For the second time that night he felt his face heating, and only hoped the blush didn't show beneath his tan. "Yes," he said, forcing his voice to be firm. "Of course, Miriam. Absolutely."

~*~

Wendy poked her head into Alexis's room. "It's free time till nine o'clock. A couple of us are going down to the creek. Want to come?"

"Yeah. That would be great." Alexis closed the journal she'd been writing and slipped it under her pillow. Marta, Sam and Rachelle were waiting for them outside the slave quarters and they walked companionably together across the meadow, which was dappled with little pink and yellow wildflowers.

It was a lovely summer evening, the sky streaking with gold and royal blue as the sun lowered itself below the horizon. The staff trainers were ensconced in what Alexis had been told was their weekly after-dinner meeting with Mistress Miriam to review trainee progress and handle various administrative details.

Alexis had completed a week of her training. Each session was a new challenge, and though she still failed more than she succeeded, Master John never gave up on her. In between sessions, she attended what was called grace training, working on the standard slave positions, as well as learning how to move with grace and beauty. Various pure

service duties were thrown in, usually with

Marta in the slave quarter bathroom. Marta was teaching her how to do the waxing, a definite step up from cleaning the toilets.

Alexis felt more alive than she'd ever felt in her life. The concept of submission was no longer just a sexy game. It had gone far beyond the slap and tickle in which she'd engaged at the BDSM clubs. She was, she thought happily, making progress. More than that, to her surprise she also found she was making friends.

She had gone straight from undergraduate school to earning an MBA, and then right into a CPA job that consumed forty to as much as eighty hours in a week, depending on tax season. As her twenties had sped by, she had, she was realizing now, rarely come up for air. This month-long vacation was a huge departure for her, and while she'd been afraid at first she wouldn't be able to handle so much time away from the office, now she realized with a startled pang of surprise that she never wanted to go back.

She found herself able to open up with the other trainees and the staff slaves in a way she never would have dreamed of doing with other women, let alone men. Back in the city she had work friends she sometimes hung out with after hours, but there had never been a girlfriend with whom she had felt comfortable enough or safe enough to confide about what she used to think of as her "kink" and now was coming to realize was a lifestyle she wasn't sure she could do without.

Marta spread a large picnic blanket over the soft grass while Sam set down a cooler filled with bottles of soda and beer. Rachelle and Alexis exchanged glances and grinned as they looked at the two trees where they'd been bound together for the predicament bondage session. Though it had only been a matter of days since that scene, Alexis felt like she'd come a long way in a short time. She wondered if Rachelle felt the same and made a mental note to talk it over with her when they were alone.

The five of them settled on the blanket, soothed by the sound of the burbling creek nearby. "This must have once been a working farm," Rachelle remarked. "A horse farm, from the look of the buildings and pastures. The slave quarters used to be stables, I reckon. I grew up on a farm down in Arkansas."

"You're right," Marta agreed. "Though the place hadn't been used for that purpose for years when Mistress Miriam bought the property."

"I love old barns like that," Rachelle said, waving her beer bottle toward the wooden structure. Its once red paint had faded to a pale pink, bleached by sun and age, and the huge old doors didn't quite close, warped by time.

"They've actually fixed it up some inside," Sam said. "There's some play equipment in there, and even a little cot. It's a great place to hide out when you need a little time alone." This remark made Alexis wonder when or why Sam would ever feel the need to hide. He seemed so supremely comfortable with himself.

He didn't elaborate, however, and she didn't feel comfortable asking, so she turned instead to

Wendy, who had stretched out next to her. "That ceremony the other night was really moving. Can I see the brand?"

"Sure." Wendy rolled to a sitting position and spread her legs to give Alexis a better view of her inner thigh. Rachelle also leaned over to examine the small infinity sign. It was still a dark red, though it seemed to be healing well.

"Hoo wee!" Rachelle enthused. "That must have hurt like hell."

"Not really." Wendy ran her finger over the sideways 8. "I mean, yeah, it hurt, but I was so excited and hopped up on endorphins, and it was over so quick that I almost didn't feel it."

The sound of Wendy's muted but agonized cry when the red-hot metal burned into her skin echoed in Alexis's mind, but she knew how the mind and body had a funny way of processing and remembering pain, and she didn't think Wendy was pretending. For Wendy the memory of the experience was that it wasn't so bad. And therefore it wasn't. That was her reality.

"You and Master John must be so in love, Wendy, to do that ritual. It was like watching a marriage ceremony, only more intense, you know? Did you meet him here at The Compound?" Rachelle asked.

"Yes. He was my trainer, in fact. I fell in love with him pretty much from the minute we met, but he was a lot slower on the uptake." She grinned an impish grin. "He's very much one for protocol, and I had to petition to be his slave, even though my training was done and I'd signed on for permanent placement at The Compound, and everyone told me he was head over heels for me. But to tell you the truth, that just made me love him more. He completes me." She frowned. "I don't mean that in a co-dependent icky way. I mean that before I met him, I wasn't fully alive, not all there, if that makes any sense. Belonging to him has made me whole."

There was a collective sigh from the others, including Alexis. Would she ever find such a connection?

"So what's your story, Sam?" Rachelle asked, interrupting Alexis's musings, for which she was grateful. She wasn't in the mood for a private personal pity party. "What brought you to The Compound? Did you train here?"

Sam reached for another bottle of beer. "I never did formally train here. I came at Mistress Miriam's request. We knew each other on the outside."

"How'd you meet?"

Alexis thought she saw a spasm of pain move over Sam's usually sunny countenance, but then he smiled. Marta put her hand lightly on Sam's shoulder and gave him a gentle squeeze. He put his hand over hers but faced Rachelle with a smile. "She and my partner used to run a dungeon in the city. I worked there too, much in the capacity I do now in the training dungeon. When Miriam moved here to start The Compound, she sold her share of the business to us. We used to visit the place, especially that first year when she was just getting started." He took a breath. "When my partner passed away three years back, she invited me to come here as a permanent staff slave. I sold the club for a nice sum and here I am." He smiled again, though Alexis saw the pain still lingering behind his eyes.

"Gosh, I'm sorry, Sam," Rachelle said, putting her hand to her mouth. "I didn't mean to pry."

"No, it's okay. I've accepted it. He was sick a long time—cancer. In the end it was better for him to go. I've made peace with it. He was the best thing I ever had, and more than most folks ever get. I'm happy here. I'm good." He took another long drink of his beer and said, "So turnabout is fair play. How about you, Rachelle? What brings you to The Compound? What are you seeking here?"

"What brings me is my fianc??, Michael Horton. When we get married, we want a 24/7 Master-slave relationship, but he says I need more training than he can give me." She laughed without a trace of chagrin. "We heard about this program and he got busy helping me write my application. The second I got accepted he packed me up and shipped me off." She shrugged, though she was still smiling. "I don't know about y'all, but I'm having the time of my life here. It's so intense, you know? But so hot, too. Master Clarence is fantastic. I'm thinking I need to get Mike's ass up here too. He could learn a thing or two about being a Master from

Master Clarence!"

Marta smiled. "Mistress Miriam says that exact thing. She says it's all very well to train submissives, but if a Dom doesn't know what he's doing, all the training in the world isn't going to matter. She's talked about starting a program for dominants, and another one for couples who want to train together. She's got a guy from Florida who specializes in training dominants who's interested in working with her to design a program. We're hoping to get it off the ground by next year."

"Well, let's get Mike signed up for the first class," Rachelle grinned. "And what about you, Marta? What's it like to belong to the head honcho? Did you go the traditional training route like me and Alexis, and then just fall in love?"

Marta beamed. "Pretty much, yeah. It was kind of ironic how it worked out. My partner sent me, much like yours, Rachelle. Looking back, it was a last-ditch thing. We had been floundering as a couple for a while. The love just wasn't there, though neither of us wanted to admit it, I guess. I signed on for a month, and when I was done and called her to come pick me up, she told me she had moved on, and she'd have my stuff shipped wherever I wanted."

"Wow, that must have hurt," Alexis said, wondering how anyone could break up with someone as lovely and seemingly perfect as Marta.

Marta smiled. "My ego maybe, but not my heart. Because, you see, Mistress Miriam had already stolen it, and I hope she never gives it back."

"So what about you, Alexis? Did someone send you here hoping to whip you into shape, pun intended?" Sam lifted his thick eyebrows.

Alexis shook her head. "I heard about this place from my play partner at a club I like to go to. I guess I wanted more, you know? You can only go so far at a club. I can only go so far on my own. I want to connect with that submissive part of me that lends meaning and worth to my sense of self, but I'm not doing so hot. I've been here a week, and I still think I suck at this most of the time."

Sam shook his head. "I've been watching you, Alexis. You're doing great. Progress, not perfection. That's my motto."

They all laughed in agreement. "Amen to that," Rachelle said with feeling.

Fireflies flitted, creating arcing sparks of light in the air, and an owl hooted in the distance. "It feels like summer camp tonight," Alexis said, feeling warm and happy. "We just need to build a campfire and get out the marshmallows."

"Speaking of summer camp," Sam said. "Remember that game we used to play as kids where everyone stood in a circle and you'd fall back into someone's arms?"

"I know that game," Rachelle piped up. "It's called Trust Fall." She scrambled to her feet. "Let's do it. I'll start."

Sam stood behind her and said, "Ready."

Rachelle crossed her arms over her chest, closed her eyes and let herself fall backward. Sam caught her in his arms and they laughed. "Your turn, Marta," Sam said.

Marta rose with that fluid grace that always made Alexis think of a ballet dancer lifting from a low curtsy. Crossing her arms over her chest as Rachelle had done, she, too, closed her eyes and sank gracefully back into Sam's arms.

"Now you," Sam said, nodding toward Alexis.

Alexis was not sure she wanted to play this game. But they were all looking at her expectantly, and so she stood slowly and approached the young man, turning her back toward him. She let her arms hang at her sides and closed her eyes. "Cross your arms over your chest, like we did," Rachelle instructed her. Alexis complied, feeling a little silly as she shifted from foot to foot. Why was she hesitating? This should be easy. Sam was strong and had already proved with the other two women that he wouldn't let them fall.

"Go on," Marta urged softly.

Alexis wanted to. And yet she couldn't. It was like there was some kind of force field at her back, holding her up, stopping her from letting go. She glanced back at Sam, who was waiting, his arms extended toward her.

"Don't think about it," Rachelle offered encouragingly. "Just do it."

The ease and happiness Alexis had felt was fast slipping away. She felt sweat prickle under her arms, and the skin on her back tingled against the invisible force field of her hesitation. She'd never been able to do this as a kid, either, she recalled now. What if Sam didn't catch her? Despite his best intentions, what if his foot slipped, or he miscalculated his position in relation to hers?

"Come on," Sam called. "What're you waiting for? Don't you trust me?"

Alexis tried to conjure the image of Master John. If he was standing behind her, would she obey? Still her body remained stiff and unyielding. How about Master Paul? She pictured his kind smile and his sparkling eyes. It didn't work.

She jumped when she felt a hand on her shoulder. Opening her eyes, she saw Marta standing beside her, and Wendy on her other side. "Sometimes you need to take baby steps," Marta said. "We'll hold you so you feel safe as you go back."

Alexis nodded, feeling both embarrassed that she couldn't do what the others had done with such seeming ease, but also warmed that they didn't want to give up on her when she'd been ready to give up on herself.

"I'm waiting," Sam said behind her. "The girls won't let you fall and I'll be here to catch you."

With their supportive hands at her shoulder and waist, Alexis let herself fall into Sam's waiting arms.

The Compound

Chapter 12

Alexis was suspended facedown about four feet from the ground, secured in a sturdy rope harness that wound around her torso and hips. Her head hung down, her long, dark hair obscuring her face. Her arms were behind her back, her legs bent at the knees so her wrists could be cuffed to her ankles.

Paul forced himself to focus on the knotwork and resist the temptation to stroke her smooth, soft skin. Miriam was right—he was professional enough not to let his desire get in the way of the training, but it was turning out to be harder than he expected.

"That should do it," John announced, stepping back from the suspended girl and gripping the convergence of rope that hung from a pulley in the ceiling. Alexis's trussed body swung gently between the two men.

Sam was at his usual post in the play dungeon, leaning against a wall where he could see all the scenes in progress, ready in case he was called for service. John gestured toward him and he came at once to their scene site. "Be on alert in case we need you."

"Yes, Sir."

John crouched in front of Alexis so his face was even with hers. "How are you? Are you comfortable? Do you feel secure in the harness?"

"Yes, Sir."

She had a nice voice. A sexy voice. Paul wondered what it would sound like in the throes of an orgasm. Not an orgasm wrested during erotic torture training, but the throaty cries of passion he would tease from her as she lay beneath him, his cock buried inside her.

"Wiggle your fingers for me," John said to Alexis. "Good. Now your toes." The trainer stood, apparently satisfied, and turned to Paul. "You can put these on while I get the rest of the stuff." He handed Paul a set of clover clamps and some lead fishing weights.

Reaching beneath the suspended woman, Paul found and rolled one of her nipples between his forefinger and thumb. He could feel it engorge and distend. Alexis moaned softly at his touch. Paul pushed away a brief fantasy of flicking the hardening nipple with his tongue and then sucking it into his mouth.

He attached the clamps to her erect nipples and knelt beside her to secure the weights that would add to the tension and heighten the erotic pain. Alexis responded with a sudden, sharp intake of breath. Paul tugged gently at the chain hanging down between her breasts, his cock hardening at her breathy gasp.

He stepped back when John returned holding a cane, a shock prod, a medium ball gag, two pairs of latex gloves and a tube of lubricant, all of which he placed on a small table near Alexis's head. John crouched again in front of Alexis, lifting her chin and looking into her eyes.

"This is endurance training. You will be subjected to both pleasure and pain. You may orgasm during the exercise. Obviously, with the gag in place you won't be able to ask permission. If you are in a situation of such extreme distress that you need the action to cease, open and close your fingers as you've been instructed before. I know how much you can take, so make sure you don't give the distress signal unless you absolutely must." He let that sink in a moment and then added, "Your intermediate goal is to take as much as you can, for as long as you can. The ultimate goal is to achieve that altered state of being where you no longer distinguish between pleasure and pain — where you surrender completely and without reservation to what we give you. Are we clear?"

"Yes, Sir," she whispered. Paul, who was standing beside her with his hand resting lightly on her back, felt a tremor move through her body.

John picked up the ball gag. "Open your mouth," he ordered. He pressed the red rubber ball into Alexis's mouth. Paul reached for her hair, lifting the thick, luxuriant tresses out of the way while John buckled the gag into place behind her head. Paul looped the hair into a loose knot at the nape of her neck to keep it out of the way.

John stood and pointed toward the items that still remained on the table. "Which do you want?"

Paul reached quickly for the cane and the prod. If just touching her nipples was enough to nudge his cock into an erection, god only knew what touching her cunt would do to him. A trace of a smile moved over John's mouth, which Paul ignored.

John moved behind Alexis and pulled on the gloves. He smeared lubricant over the fingers and placed his right hand between her legs. He placed his other hand on her thigh to hold her steady and nodded toward Paul.

"Begin," John said.

Flicking upward beneath her suspended body, Paul tapped the bound woman's breasts and the fronts of her thighs, relieved to find himself easing back into a trainer mindset. He was aware of John standing behind the bound and suspended girl, his hand buried between her thighs. He lost his concentration as he imagined the tight, velvet heat of her cunt.

Focus, he warned himself sternly. He increased the intensity of the cane strokes slowly but steadily. When he touched the live prod to her hip, Alexis jerked hard and swayed in her bonds, a muted cry gurgling behind the gag.

He touched the prod to her back, her shoulder, her calf and then resumed caning her clamped breasts, alternating between the cane and prod as the girl trembled and mewed behind her gag.

John reached for the lubricant and added some to the fingers of his left glove. He pressed a thumb into her asshole while his right hand remained buried in her cunt. Again a muted cry emerged from behind the gag. Her fingers were clenched into fists behind her back.

Paul tapped at her fists until she loosened her grip. Her back was sheened with sweat and she was trembling. Holding the cane and prod in one hand, he stroked her shoulders in a soothing motion with the other hand until he felt her relax.

John continued to frig the girl, his face a mask of concentration. Paul resumed the caning, flicking it upward beneath her body as he focused on her clamped breasts and the soft curve of her belly. He tapped at the clamps, each touch sending a spasm through her body and pulling a muted cry from her gagged mouth.

If Paul had been running the exercise, he wouldn't have gagged her, but that was John's call. Paul preferred to receive verbal input directly from a trainee. He encouraged them to talk through what was happening to them, and he could better gauge their level of distress by their cries and moans. Paul had a gentler approach overall to his training than John, but John produced excellent results, so who was he to say?

"She's coming," John said suddenly. "Don't let up."

Paul reached between the ropes with the prod, zapping Alexis's ass while tapping the cane against the tender soles of her feet. He didn't let up until she had shuddered her way through an orgasm.

Her hands, he saw, had clenched again into tight balls. She wasn't letting go. She hadn't yet surrendered. John nodded as if Paul had spoken aloud and said, "We continue. She isn't there yet."

Paul began again, tapping lightly beneath her at first, the cane just kissing the skin on her breasts and sides. As John rubbed harder and faster between her legs, Paul moved lightly on his feet around the suspended, swaying beauty. He matched John's movements stroke for stroke, alternating between the cane and the prod as John brought the girl to another climax.

Alexis stilled and hung limp and Paul met John's eyes. Was she there?

But a second later she went rigid again, her fingers clenched, a muscle flicking in her jaw, indicating to Paul she was clenching her teeth. She wasn't there. Most subs would have been there by now, floating with no resistance in a cloud of pure white light and peace, but she was resisting. Paul could almost feel her panic as if it were his own. What was holding her back?

If Paul owned her, could he bring her there?

Owned her!

What was he thinking? She was a trainee, not a

potential lover. And she was John's trainee to boot, not his. He was simply serving in an assistive capacity. His job was to cane her while John stimulated her. His job was to follow John's lead and keep his opinions and his desires to himself.

"Switch," John said suddenly, pulling Paul from his brief reverie.

"What?"

John was already pulling the gloves from his fingers. He pointed to the small table, which contained the additional pair of gloves. "Give me the cane and the prod. You make her come."

Paul took an involuntary step back, though his cock instantly rose at the thought of touching her cunt. "Let's not lose the momentum." John frowned. "Do you have a problem with touching the trainee?"

"No. No, of course not." Be professional. Keep your cool.

Paul handed the implements to John and pulled on the gloves. He moved to stand between Alexis's slender, spread thighs. The heady scent of her sex rose in his nostrils like jungle flowers and his mouth actually watered with a need to taste her musky sweetness. Her swollen cunt glistened with lubricant and her own juices.

John had already resumed the erotic torture, shocking and caning every exposed inch of Alexis's body as she jerked and twisted in her bonds. Paul ran his finger lightly over her outer labia, wishing the thin latex of the gloves didn't prevent him from feeling its silky wetness. He pressed the middle finger of his left hand into the velvet clutch of her passage and felt the muscles clamp around it. Using his right index finger, he stroked the hard nubbin of her clit with a feathery stroke until her hips began to gyrate, her entire body trembling.

"She's coming," he said, his voice hoarse. Embarrassed, he cleared his throat. John didn't let up. It should happen now. Either she was going to stop the action or she was going to fly.

John was murmuring near Alexis's ear, no doubt giving her encouragement, as he caned her breasts, making the chain between the clamps sway.

Paul moved his finger inside her heat. Come on, baby. Come on. You can do it. Let go. Fly for me.

"Now!" John shouted. "You're almost there. Give it to me."

Paul could hear the cutting whoosh of the cane and the cracking sound as it made contact with flesh. Alexis was trembling, her muscles clenched, her body bathed in sweat, a high-pitched mewling sound slipping past the fat rubber ball that pressed her tongue far back in her mouth.

She wasn't letting go. She was falling into full-fledged panic. Paul leaned forward, looking at her hands. They were clenched into fists, her knuckles white. She wasn't opening and closing them, but it was possible she was too far lost in her panic and pain to remember what to do. Again he wished she weren't gagged. He felt his anxiety rising as she writhed and jerked, swinging in the rope harness, her toes curling and uncurling.

"John," Paul said urgently. "Stop. She's not handling it. She's crashing."

John stepped back immediately, dropping the cane and the prod as he moved to stand in front of Alexis. Crouching, he leaned in close to her. "Alexis. Can you hear me?" His tone alarmed Paul, who moved quickly around the tethered girl, stripping the gloves as he went. John reached behind her head to unbuckle the gag. Her eyes were open, but their look was wild and unfocused.

"Let's get her down quick." John's voice was calm, but Paul could detect the urgency beneath it. When the gag was removed, Alexis began to cry, deep, shuddering sobs that nearly broke Paul's heart.

Though she wasn't his charge, Paul couldn't help himself. He crouched in front of her and took her face in his hands, stroking her wet cheeks as he looked into her eyes. "It's okay, Alexis. Shh, it's okay. We're getting you down."

Though she continued to cry, her eyes seemed to focus as he stared into them, and the rigid tension in her body eased a little. Sam had joined them, and within seconds they had her lowered to the mat that had been placed on the floor beneath her, her wrists and ankles free and the harness removed. She yelped when the clamps were released. Paul cupped his hands over her throbbing nipples. "It's okay," he whispered. "You're okay."

Nudging Paul aside, John bent down and lifted Alexis into his arms. Sam ran ahead of him toward the screened off area where a makeshift bedroom was set up, including a twin bed, a night stand and a chair. Paul followed behind them.

John laid Alexis gently on the bed while Sam poured a glass of water from the pitcher on the night stand. Paul was relieved to see her sobbing had subsided and her body was no longer trembling. John sat on the edge of the bed beside her and took a tissue from the night stand, which he dabbed against her red, tear-stained cheeks.

"Don't cry, Alexis. It's okay." John's voice was soothing. "It's all okay. You took a lot. I'm sorry I didn't realize it had gone too far. Did you forget the hand signal?"

"Yes," Alexis whispered. "I'm sorry. I was panicking." Her voice rose. "I don't even know what happened. Just all at once I felt like I couldn't get my breath. I couldn't tell you and I couldn't think straight. It was just too much—" Her voice broke into a hiccupping sob and it took every ounce of self-control Paul possessed not to run forward, thrust John out of the way and cradle her in his arms.

"Shh, hush now. You're safe," John said in his steady voice. "We'll try again another time. Drink some more water. A nice hot bath with soothing oils will help." He jerked his head in Sam's direction. "Sam, go find Marta and have her get a bath ready for Alexis."

His eye fell on Paul. "We're good, Paul. Thanks for paying better attention than I did. I can take it from here."

It was a clear dismissal, but Paul didn't want to go. Not until he was sure Alexis would be okay. "Alexis," he found himself saying before he realized what he was doing. "Are you okay?" It was a breach of trainer etiquette, especially after John had said he would handle the situation with his trainee.

Alexis turned her lovely, large brown eyes toward him and nodded, though she looked miserable. "Yes. Thank you, Sir. I'm sorry. I'm so sorry."

John's eyebrows were arched in surprise, his lips pressed together. But his voice remained kind, if firm, as he repeated, "We're good, Paul. Thanks."

Paul nodded brusquely, turned on his heel and strode away.

~*~

Alexis leaned back against the inflatable cushion and let the fragrant steam rise around her. Her back and ass stung beneath the water and her muscles ached as if she'd run a marathon. Her eyes still felt gritty and puffy from crying.

Marta was beside her, sitting on the wide lip of

the hot tub. She had lathered Alexis's hair and washed it with pitchers of clean, clear water she drew from the sink tap. Now she was patting Alexis's neck and forehead with a soft, wet washcloth. If Alexis hadn't felt so utterly exhausted from her ordeal, she would have been embarrassed to be ministered to in this way. As it was, she was grateful for Marta's gentle, healing touch.

"Sam told me what happened," Marta finally said in a soft voice.

Alexis said nothing for a long while. Had anyone ever fucked up as badly and as often as she seemed to?

As if reading her mind, Marta said, "You're not the first trainee to panic during a scene. You should have seen me when they did a sensory deprivation session during my first week here. I made the mistake of listing no hard limits on my application. I knew I had issues with being blindfolded and gagged, but I was convinced I could handle it. They had me bound to the spider web and when they put that hood over my head and zipped it up, I started sweating and shaking. I nearly passed out. I didn't last more than like three minutes before they called off the scene and got me out of there. The relief was so great that I started bawling like a baby, even though I wasn't hurt or in any danger. I was just so freaked out, I guess."

"Really? You?" Alexis stared at Marta's serene, composed face, trying to imagine her in full out panic mode. So even perfect slaves like Marta could fuck up? Some of the shame Alexis had been clutching around herself like a hair shirt slid away.

"Really. Me." Marta grinned, a flash of even white teeth against her smooth, dark skin. "The trainers are pretty good around here, some of the best you'll find, but they aren't mind readers. You have to communicate. You have to be honest and you have to let them know if something is going too far."

Alexis frowned, the memory of that foul-tasting rubber ball thrusting her tongue back and making her drool. "I couldn't say anything. They gagged me."

"Did you have another way to communicate? A hand signal?"

"Yeah. But that was only as a last resort. I didn't want to let Pa—I mean Master John down." She bit her lip, feeling her face heat. "I was doing okay, breathing through it, trying to flow with it, but then it started to be too much." Alexis fell silent, remembering the clamps with the weights swaying beneath them, and the explosion of pain when the tip of the cane made contact with the clamps.

"Too much?" Marta prompted.

"At first I was okay. I thought, I can do this, I can! Master John was touching me at first while Master Paul used the cane. I felt like I was getting close to whatever it is everyone talks about, but I couldn't quite get there. Then when Paul, I mean Master Paul," Alexis felt herself blushing again and she turned her face toward the wall. "When they changed places and Master Paul was behind me touching me, I thought I was going to die from the pleasure."

God, was she really saying all this stuff out loud? When she'd realized it was Paul's hands on her, in her, touching her like a lover, like her lover, every fiber of her being seemed to melt into a molten fire of pure lust.

Alexis wrapped her arms around her waist beneath the water and pressed her thighs together as she recalled Paul's fingers slipping inside her and moving over her clit, sending her almost immediately into a powerful orgasm that just wouldn't stop.

That's when it should have happened, she supposed. When the pain from the caning intertwined with the blinding pleasure of Paul's touch would meld into something more powerful than both, into that place of release and intensity that always, somehow, remained just out of her reach.

"So you were almost there," Marta said, cutting into Alexis's thoughts. "It sounds like you were very close to letting go."

Alexis snorted. "Close but no cigar. That's what my grandmother used to say." She sighed. "Maybe it's just not something I can attain." She felt a lump rising in her throat, making it hard to swallow, but she pressed on. "I've been trying, god knows I've been trying, but something always stops me. It's like there's this wall inside me and wham, up it goes, just at the crucial moment. I was hoping this experience at The Compound, this total immersion into submission and training would break down the fucking wall but..." she trailed off, tears welling in her eyes and slipping down her cheeks. "I'm sorry. I don't mean to curse." Angrily she wiped at her eyes, which were burning from too much crying already.

Marta dipped the washcloth into the water and wrung it out. "Shh, you're overwrought right now, Alexis. And you're being too hard on yourself. Lean back and close your eyes." She waited until Alexis obeyed and then placed the warm cloth over Alexis's eyelids.

"Speaking of grandmothers," Marta said, "mine used to say something that's always stuck with me. It's something that might help you as well on this journey of yours."

Alexis lifted the cloth from her eyes, for a moment forgetting how sorry she felt for herself. "Yeah? What did she say?"

"Don't quit before the miracle."

Chapter 13

Alexis sat cross-legged on her bed, her journal resting on her thigh. Part of her training was to write every day about her experiences, her thoughts and feelings. "No one else will read it," Master John had told her. "It's your private place to process what you're going through. There's no particular set of rules for what you write or how many pages you fill. It's just important that you write every day. And that you're completely honest with yourself."

During the first week her entries had been short—a few sentences describing a particular training exercise and her feelings about how it had gone. She had always considered herself more of a numbers person than a word person, and it had taken a while to get into the rhythm of writing on a daily basis. But somehow, as the days had moved into weeks, she found she had nearly filled the small leather-bound notebook. On some days she wrote for over an hour at a time or made several entries in a single day.

Though she was conscientious about writing about the progress (and sometimes the lack thereof) of her training, not all the entries were directly about that. She found herself writing about various events in her childhood that had affected her, and events at work that had stressed her out. She wrote about Master John and Wendy, and her yearning for that kind of all-encompassing connection with another human being. She wrote about the other trainees, and what she witnessed of their experiences, and how they compared with her own.

And of course, she wrote about Paul. She filled many pages wondering what he would be like as a lover, as a Master, as a partner. She mused on if he'd ever been married, and what his dreams were. She knew very little about the man, and yet she felt closer to him in some ways than to any guy she'd ever been with in an actual relationship. She often fell asleep at night with the memory of his hand on her back, or the way he had cupped her face into his hands when she'd been so panicked in the harness. She would touch her face as he had and close her eyes, hearing his voice inside her head. His words had brought her back from the brink of a scary place. It was as if he'd reached a hand directly into her soul and pulled her back into safety.

It's okay, Alexis. Shh, it's okay. We're getting you down.

There was a week left to her training, and though Master John didn't give up on her, she thought she detected a certain subtle withdrawal on his part ever since that awful day. Though maybe it was she who had withdrawn.

She worked hard, and she did well with the slave positions and grace training, but the peace and serenity she saw in others continued to elude her. She felt certain if she could just let go, she would get there. But she just couldn't figure out how.

In her heart of hearts, she secretly believed the key lay with Paul. If only he could have participated more in her training, she felt she might have broken through her resistance. But that was not to be. Master Paul had received a new trainee and she only saw him across the dungeon with his new charge, or across the table at meals. He always smiled and nodded at her, but he was busy now with someone new.

She looked down at her open journal and saw with horrified amusement what she'd been doodling on the page while her mind had wandered:

Paul Evans. Paul and Alexis Evans. Master Paul and his slave girl, Alexis. Paul. Paul. Paul.

A tap on the doorframe made her look up. Rachelle stood there, her arms crossed protectively around her torso, an anxious look in her eyes. "Hi," she said. "Can I come in for a second?"

Alexis flipped the journal closed and capped her felt-tipped pen. She patted the bed. "Sure. What's up?"

Rachelle came into the room, settling on the end of the bed. "I've got that thing tonight and I'm so nervous I could spit."

"That thing?"

"Yeah. After dinner Master Clarence is going to present me. He says I'm ready, but I don't feel ready."

"He's going to present you?" Alexis felt stupid echoing the girl, but Rachelle's words had hit her like a punch in the stomach. She thought about their shared predicament bondage scene, and how she had been the example of proper behavior for Rachelle, who had nearly pulled the double-headed dildo from them both with her lack of grace. And now she was ready for presentation? How could that be? "But you haven't even been here three weeks," Alexis blurted. "Didn't you sign on for a month, like me? I don't get it."

Rachelle nodded, furiously twirling a ringlet of her curly hair in her fingers, her face scrunched with anxiety. "I know! I need more time. I'm not ready! But Master Clarence says I am. He says I'm a natural. He says he's done what he can with me, and it's time to show the others what I've learned."

Envy and compassion warred inside Alexis. Rachelle was only, what, twenty-two? And she had arrived at The Compound after Alexis. Now here she was, ready to be presented. Master John had never told Alexis she was a natural.

At the same time, Rachelle looked so unhappy. Alexis forced herself to focus on the girl, instead of her own shortcomings. "If Master Clarence thinks you're ready, then you're ready," she offered. "I bet you'll be fantastic. Do you know what he has planned for you?"

"He's going to use the bullwhip! I'm to stand there in front of everyone, no rope, no cuffs, nothing. Just stand there with my hands behind my neck in position one, facing the audience, while he stands behind me and whips me until I fly."

"Until you fly..." Alexis repeated.

"Yeah." Rachelle nodded glumly. "I can do that when it's just me and him, with no one else paying attention, but I'm not sure I can do it in a formal ceremony. Like a command performance, you know? What if I don't get there? That bullwhip of his is wicked! I mean, he's great with it, the best ever, but it's not like a flogging. I can fly easy with a flogging. I just love the thuddy whacking against my skin. I can go in like five minutes with a good flogging. But the whip, yikes!"

"What's it like?" Alexis hadn't meant to ask, but the question had just popped out. "The bullwhip?"

"No, when you're flying."

Rachelle stopped twirling her hair and folded her hands into her lap. She sat up straighter, the nervousness about the evening's presentation draining away like water swirling down a drain. Closing her eyes a moment, Rachelle lifted her face toward the ceiling in apparent concentration. "Let me see if I can put it into words."

After a moment, she lowered her head and looked again at Alexis, her face splitting into a grin. "I'm not sure my experience is the typical one." She shrugged. "Maybe there is no typical experience. Maybe everyone's unique."

"Go on," Alexis urged softly.

Rachelle stared off into the middle distance, squinting slightly as if she could see what she was describing. "It's like a lifting into gentleness, into the middle of beautiful sunrise flames that go white. Sometimes I just sort of hover there, but other times, the really intense times, I go into this sense of running. Like I'm a four-legged creature."

Her voice had grown surer as she spoke, and her green eyes were shining. "I run so fast, without touching the ground. The wind whistles past me. It's always at night and sometimes I'm lifted higher, moving through the air with a distant awareness that something is going on far below me, but it doesn't concern me."

She broke off suddenly, looking directly at Alexis with a grin. "You must think I'm nuts, huh? Some kind of shape shifter, but that's how it is for me. What's it like for you?"

A rush of humiliation surged through Alexis, rising like bile in her throat. She looked down at her lap. "I don't know," she mumbled.

"What? You don't know how to describe it?" She patted Alexis's knee, nodding. "It is hard to put into words, I agree. Even in my journal, I have a hard time really describing it."

"No." Alexis said, meeting Rachelle's eyes, blinking back sudden tears. "I don't know what it's like. I've never done it. I don't know how."

"Oh." Rachelle's eyes slid away from Alexis, and then came back again, her smile kind. "You know, honey, maybe it's not your fault. Maybe you just haven't found the right Master."

~*~

Paul sat beside Miriam on the large sofa that faced the front of the room. Though it had been a dry summer, a weather front had moved in as the evening progressed and a heavy rain was whipping the trees outside the windows. Occasional flashes of lightning brought the branches near the windows into momentary sharp relief against the night sky. The rumble of thunder followed seconds later.

Rachelle's fiancé, Michael Horton, had flown up from Arkansas that morning. He sat on Miriam's other side, tapping his foot and causing the whole couch to shake. Miriam finally put her hand gently on his thigh and the young man's nervous thumping ceased.

"I'm so glad you could come for the presentation ceremony," she said to him. "Rachelle's blossomed here. I think you'll be pleased."

"Yes, ma'am," he replied in a thick southern drawl. "Rachelle tells me I need to come on up here and get myself some Master training." He grinned broadly and shook his head, as if the idea were absurd.

Paul lost the thread of the conversation as his eye landed on Alexis, who was kneeling up in the group of trainees along the wall. She was in the front of the line nearest the door, her lovely dark hair falling in a shiny curtain around her heart-shaped face. Trisha, Paul's latest trainee, knelt beside Alexis, at that moment leaning over to whisper something in Alexis's ear.

Alexis turned her head slightly, her eyes meeting Paul's. He smiled at her and she flushed and looked away, as she so often did when they made eye contact. Each time she did that he had to physically restrain himself from going to her, from taking her into his arms and kissing that soft, lovely mouth...

He thought often about that last session he'd been a part of, when she'd panicked and nearly gone over the edge. While he admired John's work in general, he didn't feel the fit was right between John and Alexis. Alexis, he believed, required a gentler touch. Unlike Wendy, who thrived under John's iron rule, Alexis needed someone who could gentle her into submission without causing her to retreat inside herself. Paul had come within a hair's breadth of asking Miriam if he could take over Alexis's training, but he had stopped himself, not sure of his own motives.

The room stilled suddenly, a collective hush moving through the crowd as Clarence and Rachelle entered the room. Clarence came in first, a large black bullwhip coiled in his hand. Clarence, with his dark skin, shaved head and massive shoulders, was quite a contrast to the petite young woman who followed him. Rachelle was a pretty girl, her fair skin dusted with freckles on her nose and shoulders and a mop of reddish-brown curls on her small, delicately-shaped head. She looked nervous as she turned to face the audience. But when her eyes landed on her fianc??, she broke into a broad smile and lifted her chin.

"That's my girl," Paul heard Michael Horton say in a loud stage whisper. "Ain't she the loveliest thang you ever did see?"

"Ladies and gentlemen," Clarence boomed. "Tonight is a special night. This young woman you see before you has excelled in her training and is ready to display that for you tonight. When Rachelle first arrived, she was terrified of the bullwhip. She has moved through her fear and conquered it."

He focused on the young man beside Miriam. "We are especially glad to have Rachelle's Master here tonight to witness her grace and courage." Most of the eyes in the room turned toward Michael. Paul kept his eyes on Rachelle. Though she was offering a brave smile, he could sense her tension, and see it in the clenching and unclenching of her hands at her sides.

Clarence unfurled the whip and snapped it in the air, creating a sonic crack that rivaled the thunder outside the thick walls of the old house. Several people in the room startled and jumped at the sound, Michael included. "You sure about this?" he whispered loudly to Miriam, who just nodded, again placing her hand on the man's thigh. Marta, who was sitting on the carpet at Miriam's feet, caught Paul's eye and grinned.

"Position one," Clarence said, turning his attention to Rachelle. She placed her hands behind her head and lifted her chin, her eyes on her fiancé. Clarence moved behind her and to the side, again cracking the air with the tip of the long, shiny whip. Paul had seen him use the bullwhip before, and knew what a master he was with it. He could make the tail dance like a snake, slithering over the skin with a kiss or a bite, controlled by the expert flick of his wrist.

The trainer began slowly, stroking Rachelle's ass and the backs of her thighs with the leather tail. She stayed perfectly still, her eyes on her man, only a small, sharp intake of breath or a clenching of her stomach muscles indicating she felt the lash. The tail brushed over her back and curled seductively around her narrow waist, leaving a red mark on her stomach and pulling the first gasp of real pain from the girl's lips.

Clarence returned his focus to her ass, letting the tip of the whip snap and crack against her flesh. Rachelle's lips were pressed together but she remained still, her back arched to present her large, well-shaped breasts, her red training collar snug around her throat. Clarence moved gracefully around the girl despite his bulk, the tip of the bullwhip snapping against her ass, her thigh, her breast. The room was silent, save for the crack of the whip and the rain pounding the roof and tapping at the windows.

Paul pulled his eyes from the scene and stole a glance at Alexis. She appeared riveted to the scene, her eyes wide, her body jerking slightly with each crack as if she, too, could feel the stinging kiss of the whip. He turned back to Rachelle and Clarence. Rachelle's fair skin was marked with red welts where the whip had made contact. Though the room was cool, her body was softly sheened with sweat and he could see the tremble beginning in her limbs.

Clarence leaned his head close to hers, his lips grazing her ear as he murmured something inaudible to everyone but Rachelle. She nodded slightly and closed her eyes. Paul could feel Michael Horton stiffen beside Miriam, but he stayed quiet, thank goodness. Paul could sense Rachelle was nearly there, skirting the rim of fear, sliding into the pain and letting it take her where she needed to go.

Though he'd seen it a thousand times before, it never failed to amaze Paul when it happened. He wished suddenly he was up there with her, the one to wield the whip, the one to take her to that special, intensely intimate place.

Though he'd never personally experienced flying, he had been taken along for the journey many times in the process of leading his subs there. It was almost like jumping onto a train that was lurching out of the station, and hanging on as it sped up, sharing in the exhilaration and becoming a part of it as they hurtled along the track.

Rachelle's head fell forward onto her chest, her eyes closing, her mouth going slack. She remained in position, fingers laced behind her neck, her legs strong and straight. The trembling in her body eased away and she seemed to lean into the whip's biting embrace as if it were her lover.

"Holy shit," Paul heard Michael breathe, the awe evident in his voice. Paul couldn't take his eyes from the scene. Rachelle's body was covered now in small red welts and still the whip flicked and cracked around her with Clarence's expert control. He moved with a panther's grace around the girl, the long tail of the whip like an extension of his arm. Rachelle remained still as a statue, her spirit lifted from her body and soaring somewhere in the heavens. The scene was spectacular. It was pure poetry, Paul thought, a perfect demonstration of submissive grace, as good as any he'd witnessed.

When Clarence finally lowered his arm, Rachelle remained still, her head heavy against her chest, her eyes closed. Clarence laid down the whip and moved behind her. He wrapped his dark arms around her, gently pulling her back against him. He nodded toward Michael, who stood and moved toward the stage. As if they'd arranged it beforehand, the two men lifted the naked, slender girl between them and carried her to an empty loveseat in the corner of the room.

Michael sat down first, and together he and Clarence maneuvered the girl so she was curled on his lap. Rachelle opened her eyes and smiled at her fiancé, who grinned back. "Hoo wee dog!" he cried. "You were something else up there, baby."

The room broke into spontaneous applause and warm laughter. Paul turned to see his trainee's and Alexis's reactions. Trisha was smiling and clapping along with everyone else.

Alexis was nowhere to be seen.

Paul scanned the room. Maybe she was with John. But no, John was on a chair nearby, Wendy curled contentedly at his feet, her head resting on his leg. Paul leaned toward them, catching John's eye. "Where's Alexis?"

John looked toward the row of trainees. "She's over there," he began, but stopped himself with a surprised grunt when he saw she was no longer in the line. "That's strange. She was there a moment ago. Maybe she had to use the bathroom and didn't want to disturb the scene, so she just slipped out."

Paul was relieved John didn't ask him why it was his business. It really wasn't, but her absence had taken him by surprise. John was probably right. She would return momentarily.

But she didn't.

Miriam got up and spoke a few congratulatory words to Rachelle and Michael, and thanked Clarence for his usual stellar performance, and still Alexis didn't return.

"Maybe she went back to the quarters," Wendy suggested. "It might have been hard on her, watching that performance."

Hard on her? Paul considered this. He thought about their shared session, and how hard she'd tried to fly, and how close she'd been before the panic had set in. Maybe Wendy was right. Maybe it had been hard to watch someone else slip almost effortlessly into that place, while she herself continued to struggle.

The words from her essay popped into his mind: I need help to chip away at the mortar and knock down the bricks that are hiding the true submissive within.

He should have been the one to help her. He should have been her trainer. But he wasn't. He turned to John. "You need to find her—to make sure she's okay."

John looked hard at him for a long moment and Paul suddenly realized his friend understood more than he had let on. As if to confirm this feeling, John smiled as he placed his hand on Paul's arm, squeezing gently. "You go, Paul. Go find her."

Chapter 14

Alexis stumbled as she ran, her bare feet splashing in puddles of muddy water, the rain blinding her and drenching her skin. She was crying as she ran, clutching her arms around herself as if that would provide any protection from the storm.

Watching Rachelle had been a heart-wrenching experience—so beautiful it hurt, especially because Alexis knew she would never achieve that level of grace and release. It just wasn't in her. She didn't know how to do it. For the first time in her life, Alexis had to admit she was a failure. The thought wrenched another sob from her lips.

She had been heading for the slave quarters, not caring that she would be punished for leaving the room without Master John's permission. If she had stayed in that room for one more second, she would have burst out crying in front of everyone, and that would have been her complete undoing, she knew.

But when the slave quarters loomed, she couldn't face pushing through the doors. She couldn't bear the idea of anyone seeing her in her misery and her shame, and so she kept running under the cover of darkness, her movements spurred by the flashes of lightning and the cracks of thunder. The rain poured down, the sky crying along with her as she ran.

Alexis found herself heading toward the back of the property, toward the creek where she'd shared so many happy hours with the other trainees and staff slaves. She stopped beside the old barn, breathing hard, a painful stitch in her side. She moved toward the old double doors and pulled at them. They creaked noisily open on rusted hinges. She stepped inside the dark room, relieved to be out of the torrential rain.

She stood still just inside the barn for a while, listening for the scurry of mice or the whirring of bat wings, her heart pounding, but there was only the sound of the rain clattering against the tin roof. She stood for a long while, feeling hollowed out, as if someone had reached in and scooped out her insides, leaving only misery behind.

Her eyes adjusted slowly to the room, and she saw the dim white outline of the cot Sam had mentioned. She made her way toward it and wrapped herself in the blanket that lay atop it. She had stopped sobbing, but hot tears still coursed down her cheeks, and she shivered beneath the thin coverlet. She knew she was just feeling sorry for herself.

She thought of Marta and knew she shouldn't quit before the miracle, but what if, for her, the miracle never came?

After a while the tears stopped. Her eyes burned and her heart felt like a lump of lead inside her chest.

She curled tight against herself, wondering if anyone else had ever quit the program before their training term had ended. She could spend the last week just resting in her apartment, watching old movies and catching up on her email. Or she could rent a cottage by the shore and swim in the ocean. She would put all this behind her. She would forget The Compound and Master John and Paul...

Paul.

That's what had sent her running from the room. When Rachelle had begun to fly, Alexis had turned her eyes from the scene and toward Paul. He was watching the girl with such a rapt look, leaning forward, his eyes shining as if he were watching the most spectacular sunrise, or seeing the face of his lover...

She felt as if someone had reached inside her and squeezed her heart so hard it had stopped beating. She couldn't breathe. She couldn't think. She just knew she had to get out of there. She had to get away from the sight of the man she loved staring entranced at the scene of a woman who had slipped with such apparent ease and grace into an altered state about which Alexis could only dream.

The man she loved.

Did love at first sight really exist? Was it possible to love someone you barely knew? Until she had seen Paul that very first day swimming in the pool, she would have dismissed such an idea out of hand.

But what did she know? She had never been in

love before, in her nearly thirty years of life on the planet, she had never been in love, not like this. She had been attracted to guys, sure. She'd thought she was in love, or at least edging toward it, but it had always, in the end, seemed like too much work. And if you had to work at it, was it really love?

But with Paul it was easy. All she had to do was think about him, and she felt her body soften and open inside, like a flower turning its petals toward a warm, welcoming sun. She could sense when he was near, even before she saw him. It was like a tingle in her spine, as if they were connected somehow by some invisible electric current that moved between them. His eyes were always warm when he smiled at her, and then the current would zing like a violet wand moving over her skin and it would slip inside, lighting and warming her from within.

When she'd seen Paul with his new trainee, just a day after her bungled session, she'd wanted to scream at the injustice of it. After that he'd never had time to work with Master John again. She would never be given the chance to show him she could do better.

She'd continued to do her best with Master John, but if she was honest, her heart wasn't entirely in her training anymore. She was distracted by Paul, and by the lack of him. It hurt so much to be unable to speak to him, to go to him, to let him know how she felt. Yet she hadn't dared to do any of those things. She was Master John's trainee. The rules were clear. She wasn't to fraternize with the other trainers. This wasn't, as she had to remind herself over and over, a dating service.

It was a training facility and she was here to learn, and nothing more.

Yet it had become too hard. It hurt too much to go on. She knew that with certainty now. She could no longer act as if everything was fine and hope it would somehow become reality.

Alexis had always been a woman of action. She didn't believe in putting off what needed to be done. It would be best for her to have an honest discussion with Master John, or better yet, with Mistress Miriam. Surely she wasn't the first trainee to fail. It was best to know when to cut your losses and move on.

If you go, you won't see him again.

This thought made her begin to cry again, her tears wetting the thin pillow she clutched against her cheek. A peal of thunder made her jump and give a startled cry. She heard the sound of the doors creaking open and she turned on the cot. She would have to get up and close the doors so the rain wouldn't come blowing in. Yet as she peered in the darkness, she saw the shape of a man standing in the doorway. Had Master John come in search of her? Would he punish her on the spot for running away?

Another flash of lightning lit the room and she saw it was Paul.

"Paul?" she said in a tremulous voice, forgetting to precede his name with Master, for a second wondering if she'd conjured his image in her longing for him.

"Alexis! There you are. Thank god I found you." Paul came striding into the room on those long, sexy legs of his. His long hair was wet and dripping, his shirt soaked against his skin. "You must be freezing," he said, moving closer. "There are some candles somewhere, I'm pretty sure. Let me get some light in here."

Alexis sat up, clutching the thin blanket around her as she watched in stunned silence. Paul moved toward an old chest of drawers she hadn't noticed before and pulled open the drawers, rummaging in them.

"Here we go," he said finally, striking a match with a hiss against a matchbook. He held the small flame to a candle until the wick lit. He produced three more candles, each set in a brass candle stick, and lit those as well. The space glowed with a soft, wavering light that lent a dreamlike quality to the already surreal circumstance.

He pulled something from his pocket and Alexis realized it was his cell phone. He pressed the screen rapidly with his thumbs and then slid the phone back into his pocket. Then he turned toward her, clutching an armful of blankets.

She let him take the thin, damp coverlet from her. He sat beside her on the small cot and wrapped one of the soft, thick blankets around her still shivering body. Then, to her stunned surprise, he pulled off his boots and stripped out of his wet clothing, dropping them to the ground before slipping beneath the blanket beside her.

He wrapped his arms around her, whispering against her hair, "Alexis. Alexis," making her name sound like a caress, like the softest, sweetest kiss. She could feel the length of his hard, lean body against hers, and the unmistakable rise of his cock against her thigh. He smelled so good and felt so good with his body wrapped around hers.

Tentatively she dared to put her arms around him in return, as she nestled her head between his neck and shoulder. Was this really happening? Or was this one of those lucid dreams she'd read about. If it was a dream, it was a good dream. A very good dream.

His lips found hers and they kissed, tongues exploring each other's mouths. Alexis's heart was pounding against his strong, smooth chest as he kissed her lips. "I've wanted you from the moment I saw you," he breathed into her ear between kisses. "I have to have you. Tell me it's okay. Tell me you want me too."

"Oh, Paul. Yes. Yes. Please." She knew now it was no dream, but a reality she had longed for a hundred times over the week since he'd taken her face in his hands and peered into her eyes with such loving concern.

The rain pelted on the tin roof overhead and the candles illuminated the room in a soft, flickering light. Paul rolled Alexis to her back and lifted himself over her beneath the blanket. She felt the nudge of his hard cock between her legs and she arched up, wanting him like she'd never wanted anyone before.

He held himself like that for several long beats, until Alexis thought she would die with longing. Before she realized she was speaking, the words burst from her lips. "Paul, oh god, I want you. Please, please, I want you so bad," she begged.

When he entered her, she exploded in a sudden, fierce climax, shuddering against him, stunned at the violence of her body's reaction. He pulled her close, holding her as her body spasmed in his arms, and then he began to move, his hard, perfect cock easing deep inside her wetness and then pulling back, the pleasure almost unbearable.

"Yes, yes, yes, yes," she heard herself chant in a gasping voice. He took her harder, thrusting deep inside her. The movement was perfect, his pubic bone rubbing her throbbing clit as he moved, and she began to shudder again, her cunt contracting in another series of intense climaxes. He came at the same time, his body going rigid for a moment and then jerking as he thrust inside her in hot, perfect spurts.

He collapsed against her and she could feel his heart hammering against hers. His cock still buried inside her, Paul lay still for so long she thought maybe he'd fallen asleep. She didn't mind. She loved the heavy masculine weight of him on top of her and she closed her eyes, drifting in a cloud of quiet, easy joy.

"Alexis?"

Alexis opened her eyes, for a second confused as to where she was. The old barn was still lit by candles, the scent of melted wax filling the room. The rain was falling more lightly now, just a patter against the old tin roof. Paul was lying beside her on the narrow cot, their bodies slotted together as if made for one another.

"Yes?"

"I'm sorry," he said into her hair. His arms were warm and strong around her. "It's a breach of every protocol but I just had to have you. I hope you can forgive me."

"Forgive you?" Alexis laughed in spite of herself. She twisted back in his arms to face him. "Forgive you for making the most incredible love to me? Forgive you for making my dreams come true? Are you kidding?"

He looked startled for a second and then he started to laugh, and she laughed too. All the angst and misery she'd wrapped around herself like a shroud over the past week fell away in the face of their happy, giddy laughter. Paul began to kiss her again, and she kissed him back, the laughter dying, replaced by them murmuring each other's name again and again as their bodies connected for a second time.

This time they moved slowly, the initial flare of passion now a smoldering heat that left them both sweat-soaked and exhausted by the time they were done. Again Alexis drifted in an endorphin-soaked doze.

When she opened her eyes again Paul was lifted on his elbow, smiling down at her. Reality suddenly kicked in and she struggled to sit up, a tendril of anxiety curling its way through her gut. "I better get back. Master John is probably worried. I guess I'm in a ton of trouble for running from the presentation."

Paul shook his head. "I texted him when I found you. I told him I'd take care of you. You aren't in trouble, Alexis. You're with me now. You're mine."

"Oh," she said softly, not wanting to ruin the moment by asking just what he meant by those sweeping, romantic words. The rain had stopped altogether and Alexis pushed back the covers, hot beneath them in the closeness of the barn.

"Stand up," Paul said suddenly, rolling from the cot. "Position one, hands behind your head."

Without thinking, Alexis immediately rose and assumed the position. She stood silently as Paul went to the chest of drawers, this time removing a flogger with a long, braided handle. He returned to her, leaning down to kiss her lips.

He moved behind her and began to stroke her back and ass, warming her skin with the flogger's tresses. Her nipples hardened, her cunt moistening as he brushed her skin with the sweet heat of soft leather.

He began to strike her harder, the intensity building like banked embers that burst into flame as the leather pelted her skin. The flogger thudded against her flesh from shoulder to thigh and then back again. The leather slapped against her body, the force of the blows nearly pushing her off her feet. But she stood erect and strong against the onslaught, savoring the erotic pain and letting it lift her with each fiery stroke.

She began to breathe hard, panting to get herself through the pain, which was edging from erotic pleasure into something harder to take. She felt herself sliding toward that panicked, ungraceful place and she began to dance on her toes, wondering how long she could endure this.

"Breathe," she heard Paul say behind her. "Work through it. Flow with it. Let go. Do it for me, Alexis. For us."

And then it happened.

He hit her as hard as before, maybe harder, but the panic that had threatened to spill over her ebbed away. She felt strong, as if she could endure anything, handle anything Paul gave her.

Do it for me, Alexis. For us.

"Oh," she said softly, filled with wonder. The leather still snapped against her skin but the pain was transmuting into something different. Not pleasure precisely, but a kind of interweaving between pleasure and pain that was more powerful than either experience on its own.

A curious kind of light seemed to fill her, and Alexis thought she might actually rise from the ground and float away. The only thing that kept her tethered to the earth was the steady, thudding beat of the flogger against her skin.

Her head felt heavy and suddenly she could no longer hold it up. She felt it fall back and her mouth gaped open. Her heart slowed its pounding tempo and her breathing eased into a deep, steady cadence — in...and out, in...and out — like the peaceful lull of an ocean's waves.

"Yes," she heard Paul say from a distance, as if he were far away instead of just behind her. "Yes, that's it, baby. You got it. Yes."

She drifted, vaguely aware of the steady whoosh and stroke of the leather as she skimmed the top of the calm, shining water beneath her. The sky was a brilliant blue, tiny puffs of clouds in the distance. She was filled with a peace she'd never experienced before, as every care dropped away and only joy remained.

When she came to herself again, she was once more in Paul's arms. They lay together on top of the blankets on the narrow cot. She opened her eyes to see Paul's face close to hers. He was smiling, his golden-brown eyes filled with a curious light.

"Hi," he said softly. "Welcome back."

She grinned weakly. "Where did I go?" But she knew. She had flown. It had finally happened for her. The elusive experience she'd thought she would never attain had finally come to her in a barn, at the hands of the man she loved.

~*~

Paul lay awake for a long time, listening to the steady tapping of rain on the tin roof. Alexis slept peacefully against him, her lips lifted at the corners in a small, secret smile that made him wonder what she was dreaming. He felt as if he could just lie there with her forever, suspended in the perfect afterglow of their lovemaking.

Yet he must have eventually drifted into sleep, because when he next opened his eyes it was morning. Paul stared down at the lovely woman beside him, her face softly lit by the early morning sun streaming in through the dusty barn windows. She was still asleep, curled sweetly into his arms, her soft cheek pressed against his bare chest.

Carefully he extricated himself from her embrace and eased himself quietly out of the cot. Retrieving his jeans, he pulled out his cell phone and again texted John.

"Oh my god!" Alexis shot bolt upright in the cot, her hands flying to her mouth. "I'm in trouble. What time is it? I'm going to be late for morning inspection. Master John will be waiting!"

Paul slipped the phone back into his pants pocket and returned to the cot. Sitting beside Alexis, he took her into his arms and nuzzled his face against her tousled hair. "Relax. He knows you're with me. He's not expecting you this morning."

"Oh," she said softly, and then, "and Trisha? Your trainee? Don't you need to go to her?"

He shook his head. "John's got that covered. We have the whole morning to ourselves. We need to figure stuff out, right? You and me, and where we go from here."

"Yes," she agreed.

Then she lifted her face toward his, her eyes closing and her lips parting in a clear invitation for a kiss, and Paul forgot the words he was going to say. His passion ignited with the touch of her lips against his, and he had to have her again, and then again. He had finally found what he hadn't even known he'd been searching for. And she was lying there in his arms.

Chapter 15

Miriam was already waiting for him in the small den on the first floor that she liked to use for informal meetings. A coffee carafe and three cups stood on a tray, along with a plate of blueberry scones. "Come in, Paul. John will join us in a moment." As if on cue, John appeared in the doorway.

The two men settled on chairs near the sofa where Miriam sat. She lifted the carafe in their direction. "Coffee?" John held out his cup. Paul shook his head. He felt jittery enough without the addition of caffeine. John helped himself to a scone but Paul found he had no appetite.

After Alexis and Paul had returned from the barn, he had sent her back to the quarters to shower and rest. He'd found Miriam at work in her office and they'd agreed to meet once John's dungeon session with Trisha had ended.

Paul had mentally rehearsed what he would say to Miriam and John. He would explain that it would be best for Alexis to stop her formal training with John, and see if John would be willing to take over Trisha's training until Paul could get things sorted out. He would let them know he knew this was against protocol, as Alexis still had a week to go in the contract, but given how Alexis and he felt about each other, it was the best option for all concerned.

He realized both Miriam and John were looking at him expectantly, Miriam with a small, knowing smile on her lips, John with his eyebrows raised. Paul's rehearsed speech vanished from his head and he found himself blurting, "I'm in love with her. I'm in love with Alexis Stewart. And she's in love with me."

John's eyebrows went even higher, but Miriam just continued to smile. She placed her hand on Paul's arm. "I wondered when you'd figure that out. Both of you."

Paul laughed in spite of himself, his jangling nerves settling down at last. "You knew?"

"It was hard to miss. Marta saw it too. The way you drank each other in when you thought nobody was looking. I didn't want to interfere, of course, especially during the contract tenure. I was hoping things would take their natural course after that. I guess you just jumped up the timeline a bit." Her smile edged into a grin, her eyes sparkling.

"She ran," John said, frowning. "I understand the circumstances are unusual, but she should be brought to task for such an egregious breach. She needs to be punished."

"If she were to remain as your trainee, John, I would agree," Miriam interjected. She turned to Paul.

"But she's not, is she, Paul." She said it as a statement, not a question.

Paul shook his head in agreement, marveling as he often did at Miriam's insight and understanding of human nature. "No. She wants to petition to break the contract. I — we agreed she's learned what she can from you, John." He turned to his friend. "Which was a great deal. She's incredibly grateful for all you've done for her. But something happened last night. Between us."

He leaned forward, wanting them to understand, needing them to understand. "She flew last night in the barn. It was the most incredible thing. That brick wall she talked about in her essay — the wall of resistance you came up against over and over throughout her training, John. It just" — he paused a moment — "fell away. I flogged her after we" — he felt himself blushing and knew that was ridiculous, given the circumstance, so he forced himself to continue — "made love. It was the missing piece for her, you see. She needed the intimacy of what we'd shared prior to the flogging in order to get to that place. All the training and discipline in the world wasn't going to get her there without that. She needed something more. She needed..." he paused, trying to come up with the word.

"You," Miriam supplied.

"Yeah." Paul grinned, and his heart felt as if it were filled with helium, as if he might just rise up into the air from sheer joy.

~*~

The next few weeks were a whirlwind of discussion, activity and upheaval, yet

during it all Alexis felt surer of what she was doing than at any time in her life. It felt so right, as if her entire existence had been leading to this moment, to this man, to this life.

Master John took over Trisha's training so Paul and she could focus on each other. It hadn't taken too much soul searching to recognize that she was ready to leave her old life behind. She resigned from her job at the accounting firm, ready to assume her new life as a staff slave at The Compound. Her duties would include taking over the financial management of the place, which Miriam had been handling on her own, and, according to a laughing Miriam, not well.

Alexis informed her landlord she wouldn't be renewing her lease, which as luck would have it was over at the end of the month. It was, she thought, just another sign from the universe that she was on the right path.

Back in the city, Paul helped her pack her things, and she shared the significance of this memento and that photo. They swapped stories of their childhoods, their careers and past relationships as they worked, stopping every few hours when the need for each other overtook them both.

The power and the passion between them still stunned her each time they made love. Paul claimed her not only with his body, but with the whip, with rope, with such intensity and passion it left her breathless.

"I'll never get used to this," she mused one evening as they lay in each other's arms after a particularly intense session that had left her soaring.

"Never get used to what?" Paul asked.

"To all this." She waved her hand vaguely, trying to find the right words. She found herself smiling at the sheer wonderment of it. "To you. To us. To how happy I feel now, like everything's sparkling and new."

Paul laughed. "I know. And I'll do my best to make sure you always feel that way." Pulling her closer, he dipped his head to hers and kissed her.

~*~

The night they'd been planning for had arrived. Alexis stood facing Paul in the presentation room. Though she was aware of the other people in the room — the Masters and Mistresses seated on sofas and chairs, their slaves kneeling beside them, and the row of naked trainees kneeling up along the wall by the door — she felt calm, even serene, as she gazed into the love light shining from Paul's golden-brown eyes.

It felt almost strange to be wearing clothing, having become so used to being naked while at The Compound. The long white silk dress draped softly over her body, hugging her breasts and creating a deep cleavage between them. Slits cut nearly to her hips on either side of the skirt revealed her bare legs. The fabric was sheer, accentuating rather than hiding her naked body beneath it, and she held herself proudly as she waited for the ceremony to begin.

Paul looked incredibly sexy in soft black leather pants over square-toed black boots. He wore a white silk shirt open at the throat, revealing his smooth, tan chest. Mistress Miriam rose from a sofa near the front of the room and approached the couple. She turned to face the room.

"Friends, we're gathered here this evening to share in the joining ceremony of Master Paul and slave Alexis. After the collaring, they have chosen the cane to seal their bond." She turned to them and smiled, handing each of them the gift they'd chosen for the other.

Paul went first, approaching Alexis with the slim black slave collar. She caught a glint of something gold at its center, something he must have added after their purchase. Paul held up the collar in his hands and she saw it was a small gold heart secured by a leather loop to the front of the collar.

Alexis bit her lip, blinking back the sudden tears that filled her eyes. Though Paul kept his gaze on her, he spoke loud enough so everyone in the room could hear his words. "Kneel before me," he said in a commanding voice.

Alexis sank to her knees in front of her lover and bowed her head. "Alexis," Paul continued, "with our friends as witness, with this collar I claim you as my slave, and accept the loving gift of your submission and your grace." Reaching back, Alexis gathered her hair, lifting it to bare her neck as Paul buckled the soft, supple leather collar around her throat.

Then, as they'd planned, Paul sank in turn to his knees, while Alexis rose to stand before him. She held up the gold chain they'd chosen together. She was afraid when she spoke that her voice would quaver, but it came out firm and clear. "Paul, with our friends as witness, with this chain I claim you as my Master, and accept the loving gift of your dominance, and the exchange of power that completes the circle of love between us." She clasped the gold chain in place around his neck and he rose, his eyes burning into hers.

Alexis could feel the beaming smiles of their friends around them. Paul and Alexis smiled at one another and Alexis felt as if her heart would burst with happiness.

As Paul had instructed her beforehand, Alexis slipped the straps of her dress from her shoulders and let it fall to her feet. The room quieted as Master John approached the couple holding a long, thin cane with a suede-covered handle. Alexis held out her hands, palms up, and Master John placed the cane in her hands. A ghost of a smile moved over his face as he regarded her, and then he gave a small nod in Paul's direction and returned to his seat.

Alexis remained in position, the cane balanced on her palms as Paul stepped behind her. He gathered her hair into a ponytail, using a gold ribbon to tie it before placing it over her shoulder. He returned to stand in front of her. Alexis lifted her arms higher, offering her Master the cane.

He took it and nodded, his eyes sparked with fire. "I love you," he said so softly only she could hear, and his words moved through her like strong wine, warming her to her toes.

Standing in profile to the room, Alexis lifted her arms, locking her fingers behind her neck. Paul stepped behind her. Her heart quickened as she felt the light tapping of the cane against her skin.

Though she'd flown several more times during their lovemaking over the weeks leading to this night, it had always been either with the flogger, or during a long, intense spanking, his hard hand perfect against her ass. Earlier that evening she had expressed her fear to Paul that she might not be able to slip into that altered state from the stinging cut of a cane.

"I don't want you to focus on that, darling," he'd reassured her, "That's not what tonight is about. It's about giving yourself to me completely and without reservation. If you don't fly in front of them, don't worry about it. Your focus should be entirely on me, and on the experience I give you. Your goal isn't to fly. Your goal is to submit."

Remembering his words, she took a deep breath and blew the air out slowly, feeling the mantle of her submission settle over her like a warm, comforting blanket. He focused on her ass and the backs of her thighs, the bite of the cane intensifying with each stroke. Alexis pressed her lips together, not wanting to cry out, though the steady slice of the cane was setting fire to her skin.

In spite of her fervent desire to let go, she felt herself tensing. She could feel the eyes of the people in the room on her—Master John with his implacable gaze, Mistress Miriam with her knowing smile. Arthur, her play partner from the club was there, having come all the way from the city to share in this special night. It was because of him that she'd learned of The Compound. She couldn't let him down.

She could feel the welts rising on her flesh, and the sweat pricking under her arms. She squeezed her eyes shut, her breath coming in pants. She thought of Marta, with her sweet and constant encouragement, and of Wendy, who showed such incredible courage during the branding, and of Rachelle, who had flown with such ease and grace beneath Master Clarence's loving touch.

"I love you," Paul murmured softly, his lips brushing her ear.

At that moment Alexis felt the room fall away. Anxiety, expectation, anticipation melted away beneath the heat of Paul's love. For the first time that evening Alexis felt herself truly let go.

The bite of the cane was no less intense. If anything, Paul was striking her harder than before, each cut preceded by the whipping sound of rattan arcing through the air the split second before contact. Yet she could feel the pain ebbing away, and all at once she felt herself lifting, her spirit leaving her body to glide with perfect grace over the vast, deep blue of an endless ocean. She could feel the sun warm on her back, and the embrace of the warm water enveloping her.

Her head fell back, her lips parting, her heart slowing, beating in time to each biting, perfect stroke of the cane. She was vaguely aware that the caning continued, but she no longer registered the pain. Or more precisely, she welcomed it, taking it deep inside and spinning it outward into a pure, white light that filled her with utter peace and a quiet, barely contained joy.

~*~

Paul lowered the cane, letting it drop softly to the carpet. He could feel the collective awe around them as they watched the lovely woman, who stood still as a living statue, the only movement the slow rise and fall of her breathing. He moved closer, feeling the heat of her skin as he wrapped his arms around her from behind. She leaned back into him, letting her full weight fall against him.

Paul bent down and placed one arm behind her knees, scooping Alexis into his arms. He carried her to the loveseat that had been set aside for just this purpose, and lowered himself down into it. She opened her eyes slowly, as if waking from a long, restful sleep. As her eyes focused on his face, Alexis broke into a smile filled with such joy and pleasure that Paul thought his heart would crack.

They both turned their heads at the sound of

champagne corks popping. John and Wendy approached, each carrying two glasses. Paul helped Alexis to a sitting position beside him, and they each took an offered glass.

John raised his glass in a toast. "To Alexis, who has joined the unique family that is The Compound." John winked at her as the four of them clinked glasses. "Good job, kiddo."

Wendy added, "To Miriam, who created a place where dreams really do come true." Paul turned to Alexis, eyes only for her, as he added softly, "To us."

And all at once she understood.

All her life she had yearned for true submission, and sought it in the wrong places, again and again and again. She would have continued to fail, she realized now, no matter how well trained she became, no matter how intense her desire to succeed. For her, the need and ability to submit weren't enough, and never would be. For her there had to be more. There had to be love.

Love was the key.

Here's a sneak peek at **Beyond The Compound – Book 2 of The Compound Trilogy**

What readers are saying - "A great read for BDSM lovers..." "Totally HOT! I loved it!" "Filled with hot sex, self-discovery and a fantastic ending!"

Chapter 1

The slave stood perfectly still, arms raised high over her head, crossed at the wrists. Her eyes seemed turned inward, as if she were lost inside a dream. The only hint she was suffering, indeed, that she was even aware of what was happening to her, was the slight wince that moved like a whisper of wings over her features when the whip found its mark.

The Mistress stood to the side of the slave, who faced George in all her naked splendor. Her breasts were marked with a pleasing pattern of thin red lines left behind by the perfectly aimed strokes of the whip. When the tip caught her nipple, a small sigh escaped the woman's parted lips and a tremor moved through her lithe form.

"Focus," Mistress Miriam commanded in a low, clear voice. She struck the other nipple with the knotted tip of the whip, and the slave girl's composure slipped a little more. She bit her lower lip and George could see the sheen of perspiration on her face and throat. "Remember why you exist," the Mistress intoned. "You were born for this, Hailey. Let the pain take you where you need to go."

The slave girl nodded slightly, serenity once again suffusing her delicate features. She had a narrow face, large dark blue eyes and shoulder-length blond hair, the kind that wasn't any one color, but more like a blend of pale ash, buttery yellow and shimmering gold.

"Turn," the Mistress commanded, and the woman pivoted slowly, arms still raised and crossed over her head. Christ, her ass was perfection itself — two round, lush globes absolutely made for spanking. George shifted on the sofa, using the contract he held in his hands to hide his sudden erection — not that anyone was looking at him.

The other bidder was focused squarely on the two stunning women in front of the huge stone fireplace. He didn't look much over forty, no gray yet in his slicked-back blond hair. He looked like one of those Wall Street investment banker types dressed down for the weekend, consciously casual in rumpled linen pants and Gucci loafers with no socks.

George shifted his gaze back where it belonged. The slave girl was now panting, making sexy little sounds not unlike a woman nearing orgasm, as if the whip were a cock, instead of leather, and stroking her cunt, instead of brutally marking her ass and thighs. She wasn't merely enduring this whipping with grace—she loved it. She craved it. She was perfect. He had to get her, no matter the cost.

Finally Mistress Miriam lowered the whip. "You may thank me," she said imperiously, and the girl, her entire body trembling, lowered herself as gracefully as a ballerina to the floor and pressed her pretty mouth to the toe of Mistress Miriam's shoe.

Mistress Miriam stepped back. "Kneel, at ease, facing the gentlemen," she commanded. The girl lifted herself so her back was straight. Still on her knees, she pivoted so she faced the room. She rested her hands, palms up, on her thighs, her eyes appropriately downcast, though George could see the strength in her bearing and pride in the lift of her chin.

That was all to the good. George had never favored timid, simpering women. He liked them strong and sassy—all the more fun to whip them—metaphorically and literally—into shape. At the same time, she had to be willing and eager to accept whatever devious torture her Master's active imagination and even more active libido could devise. What's more, she needed to know how to keep her mouth shut, not only during her tenure, but afterward.

George glanced down at the contract he held in his hands. Six months—the timeframe was a little long, and the starting price a little steep, but it was still within budget. The girl, of course, was disease free and also on birth control, a definite plus. Naturally he'd had to provide a clean bill of health as well. Everything else looked to be in order. No question, The Compound ran a first class operation.

George, an attorney by profession, though he no longer actively practiced, was aware this contract would never withstand the scrutiny of a court of law. It was illegal to sell one person to another, even if that person was complicit in the sale and would be handsomely paid at the end of the term. You weren't allowed to buy a sex slave and keep her under lock and key, there solely to do your sexual bidding and accept whatever erotic tortures you chose to mete out.

No matter — no courts would be involved in the process. George knew the slaves trained at The Compound received the finest education in the art of erotic submission, which included absolute obedience. In a word, Compound slaves knew to keep their mouths shut.

Another naked beauty, one of The Compound's staff slaves, glided silently into the room, carrying a bottle of the very fine Cognac she'd served them earlier in the evening. The second bidder held up his brandy snifter and the girl poured. George shook his head at the offer to replenish his glass — he was working and needed his mind clear.

Mistress Miriam sat in a chair across from George and the other bidder and crossed one long, perfect leg over the other. "As you can see," she said, "slave Hailey can take a very solid whipping with grace and courage. She is also highly sexually responsive, and extremely capable of serving a man's every sensual need and desire. Hailey craves intensity of experience. She needs a Master who will challenge her and take her to the edge of her limits and perhaps a bit beyond."

The girl remained still as a statue, a small, secret smile playing over her pretty lips. She was so young and beautiful — why would she sell herself like this to some old man she'd never met?

Money, of course. It made the world go round.

Which wasn't to say he wasn't quite impressed with what he'd seen. The tour of the facility supported the stellar reputation The Compound had garnered over the past years in the international BDSM community. Though they'd been around less than a decade, The Compound was known for producing highly trained sex slaves and placing them with carefully screened Masters around the world, and unlike some groups he'd been involved with, the slaves actually received a significant portion of the proceeds.

Maybe Mistress Miriam really did give a shit what happened to the girls she placed, but even if her motives were primarily altruistic, she was running a business. She could spout all the lofty sentiments she wanted about the art of erotic submission, and the grace and courage of their highly trained slave girls, but in the end the girl would go to the highest bidder.

"Would either of you care to examine slave Hailey before we begin the bidding?"

The other bidder rose to his feet, his eyes fixed hungrily on the naked, kneeling girl. "Yes."

Mistress Miriam turned to Hailey and lifted one eyebrow, which was apparently enough of a command to cause the girl to rise to her feet in a fluid, sensual motion that made George's bones ache with desire.

The guy strode to the front of the room. He moved with the kind of confident determination of someone used to being in charge. He stood in front of the slave girl, but George was enough off to the side that he could see what the other bidder was doing. He lifted his hand, and for a second, George thought he was going to slap the girl, but instead he gently cupped her cheek and murmured something George couldn't quite catch.

His hand slid down her cheek to her throat, his fingers gripping her just below the jawline. Hailey's pupils dilated and her lips parted. It was clear the guy was pushing some submissive buttons with his sensual chokehold.

He let her go and stepped back a little. Gripping one of her lovely nipples between forefinger and thumb, he gave it a sudden, savage twist. The girl rounded her lips into a pretty O, but otherwise made no protest. The guy slapped at her thigh and she widened her stance, bare feet flat on the stone hearth.

Again he murmured something George couldn't

quite catch. The girl tilted her pelvis forward, her face outwardly serene, though George couldn't help but wonder what was going on in that pretty head of hers.

The man gripped her vulva like he was grabbing a piece of fruit. He must have been doing something with his fingers, judging by the pretty pink blush that moved over Hailey's throat and cheeks and the way her head fell slightly back. "Oh," she breathed, the word like fingers stroking George's cock. This one would be a prize, no question about it.

The second bidder withdrew his hand and nudged the girl's shoulder. She pirouetted so her back was to them, and George fondled that perfect ass with his eyes, even as the man used his hands to do the same thing. Finally the man returned to his seat.

Mistress Miriam turned to George. "And you, Sir?"

George shook his head. He'd seen all he needed to know. The girl was perfect. He cleared his throat. "I'm good, thanks."

"Slave Hailey," Mistress Miriam said, "you may wait in my office."

"Yes, Mistress," the girl said softly. Her voice was low and throaty, and George wondered how she'd sound in the throes of orgasm.

Once the girl was gone, Mistress Miriam faced the two men. "As we've previously discussed the contract has a six-month tenure, with a renewal clause at the end of the term. The initial bid is two hundred thousand dollars, half to be paid up front to The Compound, the other half to be maintained in an account for the slave until the end of her term of service. As you know, we don't generally have bidding for our contracts, instead usually matching a particular Master with a particular slave for an agreed upon price. But since you both seem intent on procuring this particular slave, I've decided this is the most equitable solution to the issue."

And the most profitable for you, George thought, though of course he didn't say this aloud.

"Two fifty," the other bidder promptly said.

"Two sixty," George rejoined.

"Two seventy."

"Two eighty."

The other bidder was silent for several beats, and George imagined he was calculating how much of a bonus his bank would give him that year, and if Hailey was worth the price. The guy brought his hand to his face, the hand that had been buried in the beauty's cunt a moment before and closed his eyes, as if inhaling her sensual perfume. Apparently it was enough to push him to the next step.

"Three hundred," he said, casting a triumphant look in George's direction, as if to say, top that, old man.

You bet your ass I will, George silently responded. The guy had no clue who he was up against. Time to end this thing.

"Three fifty," George said softly, his eyes fixed on Mistress Miriam.

Silence for several beats. George kept his eyes on Mistress Miriam, each passing second a small triumph. Going once, going twice…

"If that's the final bid…" Mistress Miriam said, letting the sentence trail away.

George finally permitted himself to glance at his competition. The guy pressed his lips into a thin line and George could see the struggle on his face. He wanted the girl, but the price was too steep. Finally he gave a small, sharp shake of his head.

Victory!

Mistress Miriam stood and extended her hand to George, who stood as well, trying to keep the goofy grin from his face. "Slave Hailey is one of the most highly trained and deeply submissive slaves The Compound has ever produced," she said as she gripped his hand with her long, cool fingers. "I think you will be very happy."

Yeah. I'd be delirious with joy, George thought wryly, if only she were for me.

~*~

Hailey cast a sideways glance at the man sitting beside her as they winged their way across the country in the first private jet Hailey had ever been in. He was a good-looking guy for his age, which she guessed was somewhere in the mid fifties. He had a thick head of silver hair, clear blue eyes, a still firm jaw and craggy features. But if she were honest, she had to admit she'd been rooting for the younger Master.

No point in wasting time on what might have been, so she put the thought out of her head. She would focus instead on doing the best she could for the man who had chosen her. Age not withstanding, Master George seemed honest, kind, and serious about the lifestyle, all of which were excellent points in his favor.

After two months of intensive training at The Compound, and a lifetime of searching for, and as yet never finding, a true Master who would make her his own, Hailey had given herself over to the process. Though she recognized the artificiality inherent in placing herself under contract to a virtual stranger, at the same time she trusted Mistress Miriam to place her with someone of integrity and quality.

She needed a Master who would intuitively understand and respect her deep-seated longing to submit—body and soul—to another person. She needed someone as dedicated and committed to the lifestyle as she was. In hindsight, it was evident in the past she'd made a mistake in seeking a lover who was dominant, rather than a Dominant who might in time become a lover. True that wasn't likely to happen with this man who was old enough to be her father, but that was okay. She would learn and grow from the experience, and hopefully make him happy and proud to own her for the duration of the contract. After that — who knew?

Energized by her internal pep talk, Hailey decided to begin their new relationship by telling Master George she was honored to have this opportunity to serve him, and would make every effort to give him the best of her submission.

"Permission to speak, Sir?" Hailey ventured.

The man turned to her, as if surprised by the question. "You don't need permission. Not with me."

Had she heard him correctly? "I'm sorry, I don't understand, Sir."

He smiled. "Listen. Now that everything's wrapped up and we're on our way to your new life for the next six months, I need to level with you, Hailey."

A sliver of unease sliced its way through Hailey's gut. Surely the time to level, whatever that meant, had come before they were headed across the country, where she'd promised to serve as his personal sex slave for the next six months? Hailey willed herself to remain calm. Slaves were patient. Slaves didn't anticipate — they accepted. She waited, her eyes fixed on Master George's face.

He blew out a breath, as if steeling himself for what he had to say. "I'm afraid I've procured you under false pretenses."

"False pretenses?" Hailey echoed, thoroughly confused and unsettled by this admission.

"Mistress Miriam was aware of the arrangements," George continued, "but I didn't mention them to you until now because discretion is of the utmost importance to my client. I did buy your contract, or rather, I negotiated its purchase, but I'm not the one who will own you for the next six months."

Hailey realized she was clutching the armrests of her seat with a white-knuckled grip. Willing herself to relax, she moved her hands into her lap and folded them together while her mind struggled to process what the man was saying.

"The person who bought you doesn't like to make himself a target for the public. He's a very private man in his personal life. That's why he couldn't come himself, much as he would have liked to. I'm his personal representative in certain transactions. He's — well, you'll see when you meet him."

Even while Hailey's mind was trying to let go of the idea that this kind, older man would not be her Master for the next six months, she was deeply intrigued by what he was saying. Who was this mystery man she was being delivered to?

Someone famous. It had to be. But why not just tell her? And even if the guy was some kind of celebrity or big shot, why go to such lengths? It wasn't like anyone at The Compound would care who the guy was, surely? They were part of a BDSM community that understood the need for discretion. Folks seriously committed to the lifestyle were well aware of the discrimination, intolerance and basic misunderstanding that existed out there.

Unless — oh shit — what if the man she signed her life away to for the next half year was one of those fanatical, pseudo-religious types? Someone who couldn't risk showing his face in a so-called den of iniquity? One of those smarmy creeps who amassed a fortune by preaching against sinners like homosexuals and other deviants, and then were caught with their pants around their ankles, their cocks down another guy's throat? Someone who would spend the next six months forcing Hailey to atone for her "sins"?

What the hell have I done?

The sliver of unease bloomed into a fist of panic that clutched at Hailey's gut. She closed her eyes and drew in and then released a deep, cleansing breath. She called on all her grace and submission training, bringing it around her like a warm, comforting cloak. Stay calm. Don't jump to conclusions. Mistress Miriam would never place you with someone like that. Whatever happens, submit with grace and courage. Accept what is offered, and serve with passion.

"Hey," Master George, or was he just George, said gently, placing a hand on her shoulder. "You okay? You're looking a little pale. Are you motion sick?"

Hailey opened her eyes and forced a smile. "No, thank you. I'm okay. Just still not really clear on what you're telling me. I'm trying to adjust to this change in plans. I thought you were the one who bought me."

A spasm of pain seemed to move over the man's face. "Don't I wish," he said in an undertone so that she barely caught the words.

She had to know what was going on, and so she pressed, "Do I know this person you're taking me to? Can you tell me his name?"

George seemed to ponder the question. "Okay, you're right," he finally said. "You deserve to know, and anyway, you'll know soon enough. It's Ronan Wolfe. That's who bought you."

Hailey struggled to place the name. An actor. That was it. He was in the movies. Which explained why they were headed out to California. Yes, he must be an actor, though for the life of her, she couldn't conjure a face to go with the name.

At twenty-eight, Hailey knew she was definitely in the minority in her generation. A yoga teacher by profession, she didn't own a computer or a television. Her cell phone wasn't smart at all. She rarely went to the movies, and in fact couldn't remember the last time she'd been to one. She vastly preferred to lose herself in a good book, or in peaceful meditation beside the creek at the back of her cottage in her small Vermont town.

George was regarding her expectantly, and so she said, "He's an actor, right?"

His expression went from confusion to incredulity to amusement within the space of a few seconds. He burst out laughing, a big guffaw that made her smile back in spite of herself. "Good one. You had me going for a second there."

Hailey was confused. "You mean he's not an actor?"

George tilted his head, his eyebrows lifted in disbelief. "You mean you honestly don't know who Ronan Wolfe is? The biggest heartthrob of the decade? The man who's been described as Gregory Peck, Paul Newman and George Clooney all rolled into one incredible package of artistic talent and devastating good looks?"

"I'm sorry," Hailey replied lamely. "I don't go to the movies much."

"I guess not. Or watch TV. Or live in the modern world." His tone dripped with sarcasm and Hailey felt herself coloring. She looked away so he wouldn't see her blush.

"I'm sorry." George's tone had changed to one of contrition. She felt his hand again on her arm. "That was uncalled for." George gave a small laugh. "I should be impressed to be with the one straight woman in America who doesn't fall into a dead faint at the prospect of meeting Ronan Wolfe in the flesh."

Hailey offered an apologetic shrug, not sure what to say. If this guy was as famous as all that, she would surely recognize him when she saw him, she supposed. The prospect of serving a man who probably had an ego the size of Montana wasn't exactly thrilling, but he was clearly serious about owning a trained submissive, given all the trouble he'd gone to in order to procure her.

Unless... Unless he just had more money than he knew what to do with, and had jumped on the BDSM bandwagon as something kinky and fun to try out? Was she being consigned to spend six months with a dabbler in the scene? A vapid, clueless celebrity looking to explore a casual kink?

True, the money was great—she would pocket more from this six-month contract than she earned in five years as a yoga instructor—but money hadn't been her primary motivator when she signed on for training at The Compound. She was seeking a true connection with a bona fide BDSM Master. The idea of being a casual play toy for some wannabe Dom was not appealing, even if he was god's gift to women.

"Is he serious about the lifestyle?" she ventured. "I mean," she added hastily, "I don't mean any disrespect, but is Mr. Wolfe just, um, you know, just doing this for fun? Has he done anything like this before?"

"You can rest easy on that score, Hailey. I've known Ronan for a long time, and he's no lightweight looking for a bit of slap and tickle. He's heavily into the scene, and though I'm not sure he's looking for love"— George offered a wry smile as he said this—"he's as serious as you are about BDSM."

Hailey let out a breath she hadn't realized she'd been holding. "The thing is," George continued, "because of who he is, and the work he does, he can't really afford to have it out there that he's into the lifestyle. The press would have a field day if they found out the guy was into whips and chains, which is how they would characterize it. Ronan's a very private guy, and he doesn't want his private business to become fodder for the gossip mills. I'm sure you heard about his big breakup with Jennifer St. Claire and that whole mess a few years back."

Hailey opened her mouth to say yes, of course, as she desperately tried to summon up who Jennifer St. Claire might be, and George laughed again. "Oh, right," he said, still chuckling. "I forgot. I'm dealing with the one woman in the country who doesn't give a shit about Hollywood royalty." He patted her knee. "Anyway, the press had a real field day with that one, and most of what they reported had zero basis in fact, but they didn't let that bother them, of course. Can you imagine what they'd do if they found out Ronan had a live-in, trained slave girl?"

Hailey could only imagine. She didn't particularly relish the idea of being splashed across the tabloids either. Though she wasn't ashamed of her submissive leanings or lifestyle, she did live in the real world, too, and had no desire to be embroiled in any kind of scandal.

They were quiet for a while, and Hailey was glad for the silence as she tried to collect her thoughts and feelings. Master George was just George — a procurer for this famous but reclusive celebrity who was seeking a sub girl, but not love.

Okay, fine. It was better to be prepared in advance for what she was getting into, and though she would have appreciated knowing these facts before she'd signed on the dotted line, would her decision have been any different if she'd known the truth?

Her first and best yoga and meditation instructor, Deirdre Levy, used to say something to Hailey when she experienced a setback in her progress or hit a roadblock of some kind. "Remember, dear heart," her mentor would tell her with a kind smile, "everything happens for a reason and a purpose, and it serves you."

Hailey had never entirely bought the concept that everything happened for a particular reason — there was definitely bad, random shit out there in the universe that could smack you in the face and hurl you to the ground. This was brutally confirmed in Hailey's mind when Deirdre died later that year of ovarian cancer at the absurdly young age of forty-two.

But she did like the concept of taking those random events, both good and bad, and figuring out how they could serve her. Whatever happened in California, it was up to Hailey to make it work. Not to make the best of it in the sense of submitting to a fate beyond one's control, but rather to learn from whatever happened, to grow from it and take something good from it.

Finding out about The Compound from a dear friend in the scene, and then getting accepted for the training, had been both the best and most challenging experience of Hailey's life.

Until now.

Somehow she had a feeling these next six

months would prove even more of a challenge. But she would make it serve her. She would rise to the occasion. She would serve Master Ronan with all the passion and courage she possessed. And she would put that lingering thought of finding true love aside for now.

The flight attendant, a pleasant young man named Carlo, appeared carrying a tray loaded with fresh fruit, various cheeses, bread and crackers, plus two bottles of Perrier water, all of which he set on the table between their large, comfortable seats. "Some light refreshment for you," he said with a professional smile. "We should be arriving in about two hours."

He picked up the bottle of champagne that he'd left chilling in a bucket of ice on a side bar. "Would you care for some champagne?"

"I most certainly would," George said enthusiastically. He turned to Hailey. "How about you?"

"I would love some."

Carlo popped the cork and poured the sparkling wine into two crystal flutes. "Do let me know if there's anything else," he said, and then disappeared.

George lifted his hand in a toast, and Hailey clinked the edge of her glass to his. "To youth and money," he said with a wink. "If I had either, I would make you my own." He laughed, another big guffaw, and then downed his glass in one gulp.

The Compound

www.ingramcontent.com/pod-product-compliance
Lightning Source LLC
LaVergne TN
LVHW020059280126
830614LV00029B/559